Mary Greene Ware

Thoughts in My Garden

Mary Greene Ware

Thoughts in My Garden

ISBN/EAN: 9783337090579

Printed in Europe, USA, Canada, Australia, Japan

Cover: Foto ©Andreas Hilbeck / pixelio.de

More available books at **www.hansebooks.com**

THOUGHTS IN MY GARDEN

BY

MARY G. WARE.

AUTHOR OF "ELEMENTS OF CHARACTER."

"The human mind is as ground; which is such as it is made by cultivation."
SWEDENBORG.

BOSTON:

CROSBY AND NICHOLS,

AND

WM. CARTER & BROTHER.

1863.

BOSTON:

CHAS. H. CROSBY, PRINTER, 5 & 7 WATER STREET.

CONTENTS.

INTRODUCTORY ESSAY.

"What surmounts the reach
Of human sense I shall delineate so,
By likening spiritual to corporal forms,
As may express them best; though what if earth
Be but the shadow of heaven; and things therein
Each to other like, more than on earth is thought?"

MILTON.

INTRODUCTORY ESSAY.

THOSE among the readers of this little volume who are not familiar with the doctrines of the New Church, as taught by Swedenborg, may look upon the explanations contained in it of the correspondence of things natural with things spiritual, as fanciful or poetical merely, instead of being what the writer intended, strictly scientific. To such, a more systematic statement of the subject may be interesting and useful.

There has always been a class of minds not willing, or not able, to rest patiently in the external knowledge of the material world, but seeking earnestly to find some meaning hidden within, some *anima mundi*, informing with wisdom the dead matter of which earth is made, and the living organisms, vegetable and animal, that cover its surface. So, too, ever since the promulgation of the Scriptures, a similar class of minds has been seeking there for a sense within the letter, a hidden wisdom, that shall give to the seemingly strange symbolism of the Word a meaning and a power that it must ever lack to the reader who is destitute of such knowledge.

Various theories aiming to explain the spiritual system of the universe and of the Scriptures, have been given to the world; but none that has been widely received. It is evident that no human mind can be competent to explain the wisdom and the love of the Divine Mind, as a whole, though it may attain to many detached and fragmentary truths. Divine illumination must be needful, in order that the human intellect should have breadth and depth to measure and to fathom divinity. Swedenborg claims to have received such illumination, for the purpose of teaching mankind the internal meaning of the Word and Works of God. Strong internal evidence that he did so, lies in the fact that his exposition of the doctrine of correspondence is a positive science, reducing the Word and Works to perfect con-sistency in themselves, and perfect harmony with each other. In the light of his teachings, the supposed contradictions of science and religion

Wisdom or Love. It is a form or expression of either truth or goodness. Thus all things come into one or the other of two great classes, which correspond to one or the other of these two universal attributes of the Heavenly Father. Innumerable as are the forms of creation, they still all come under one or the other class; all come from the Divine Love or Wisdom, all correspond to some form of goodness or truth, all address themselves either to the affections or the thoughts of man.

It must not be supposed that by correspondence is meant resemblance in the way we mean when we say one person or thing looks like another person or thing. Perhaps no better illustration can be given of what is meant than the human countenance, which, in its ever-varying expressions, corresponds to the emotions of the soul. As the human features offer to the eye something which expresses the varying passions of the mind within, so the universe of matter expresses or corresponds to all that is in the soul of man, and the universe of spirit all that is in the soul of angels. As men and angels are formed in the image and likeness of God, these two universes correspond also to Him, and so aid men and angels to come nearer to Him through the instruction they gain from these correspondences. The universe thus forms the Grand Man, which is the basis of the whole system of correspondences.

First there is God, the Infinite, Divine Man. Then there is the finite, angelic man, formed in His image, with a spiritual world about him corresponding to his being, adapted to his wants, and capable of educating his faculties to the utmost. Then there is man in his lowest state, still in the likeness of God, but clad in a material form, and dwelling in a material world; corresponding to his being, adapted to his wants, and capable of opening his faculties, and preparing them for that higher training which awaits him, when, putting off his material frame, he enters upon the spiritual world, with the nicer senses, the wiser thoughts, the purer affections that pertain to the angel.

Thus from the Divine Humanity downward through angels and men, and all the things that surround them, all tend to the human form, all join to make up the Grand Man, or macrocosm, of the universe. Everywhere and always men and angels are surrounded by types, the whole value and purpose of which is to help them to the comprehension of themselves and of their Creator;

to teach them spiritual truth, by means of which they may be constantly ascending to a higher degree of spiritual life.

The human soul, clad in a material body and placed in a material world, finds its true life only when it learns to perceive that the material is the result of the spiritual, and that it exists only through its correspondence with the spiritual. The material world does nothing but mislead us, until we know and feel that it is entirely secondary to the spiritual world. Then it becomes a ladder on which we may mount up to the highest wisdom of which man is capable.

The science of correspondences is the one absolute and universal science, for it includes all natural and physical science, all art and literature, all philosophy and theology, all thought and feeling.

The old theology taught that the higher we ascended in the spiritual world the less complex everything became. It asserted that God was a simple entity, without parts or affections; that angels were intangible creatures, without organized forms; that heaven was an insubstantial, cloudy place, in which these beings floated, singing eternal anthems of praise to the glory of the

Almighty. Yet this life and these beings were asserted to be perfect and happy beyond anything that man could conceive.

Everything that we see on earth reverses all this ; for here we find that the capacity for knowledge and for happiness increases in direct proportion with the complexity of organization of the being. From the soft, scarcely organized mass of the mollusk, through fish, reptile, bird and beast, up to the firm, delicate, and exquisitely complex organization of man, the capacity for use, for culture, and for enjoyment, rises proportionately higher and higher. Is it not then irrational to believe that when we pass from man to angel we become less highly organized, less perfect in form, less sensitive in perception? We believe that a true analogy indicates what the New Church teaches ; that the angel retains all that made the man capable of using his material form. That the spiritual body permeates every fibre and atom of the material body ; and that when the material body falls off, the spiritual body remains in a similar form, but more perfect in every sense, capacity and power ; thus becoming a fit instrument for the use of the soul in the higher world on which it is entering.

The spiritual world is the soul of the natural world, as the spiritual body is the soul of the natural body. The natural body and the natural world exist only because the spiritual body and the spiritual world are within them; and they die and decay so soon as the spiritual is withdrawn from them.

A man with only the sense of touch would grope about the world perceiving only the objects he can reach by actual contact with his body, and perceiving them in a very imperfect way. If the other senses could be opened to him one after another, the added perceptions of each would seem like the entering into a new world, so much would be offered to his observation with each new power of perception. The worlds of smell and taste, of sight and sound, would each seem like a new revelation; and yet they were all about him just as perfectly before he had the use of his senses as after. Just in the same way the world of spirit is all around us while we live in the world of matter; but our senses are not yet opened to perceive it. The death of the body is the opening of the spiritual senses, by which we shall be made capable of perceiving the glories and perfections of the spiritual world. Just in proportion as that

2

world is more perfect than this, must its objects of
sense be more complex, varied and numerous;
and our perceptions more delicate, our capacity of
enjoyment more exquisite.   That our moral nature
may find scope for the employment of its faculties,
there must be the most varied social relations in
which all charity will become mutual; each angel
having something to give his neighbor, and some
want which his neighbor may supply.   As in the
human body each part is dependent on every
other part, while it has its own special function in
relation to the whole, so in the Grand Man of the
spiritual world each individual is made happy by
fulfilling the duties of his own sphere, and receiving in turn the benefits that belong to him.   No
one there desires to leave his own place, to escape
from his own duties, or to receive what does not
belong to him; yet the places, the duties and the
gifts are more varied and more numerous than we
can conceive.   As we cannot imagine one sense or
organ of the human body envious or jealous of another, because no one sense or organ can do the
duty of another so agreeably to itself as it can do
its own, so in heaven as happiness consists, for
the most part, in the doing of duty, each angel
wishes to do what he is best fitted for doing well,

and each is placed where his own special duty is to be done.

What the duties of the spiritual world are we are not told. They are not the same as those of earth, but they correspond in the benefits which they confer upon the spiritual body to those of earth in what they do for the natural body. As the spiritual body is immeasurably more varied in its capacities and in its wants than the natural body, so the employments of the spiritual world will be more varied than those of earth.

Rising above the heavenly hosts to the contemplation of the Deity who created and who sustains the universe, holding all things from the highest to the lowest, from the greatest to the most minute, in the embrace of His Almighty power, is it rational to believe that this being of infinities is a simple entity, without parts or affections, an abstract "somewhat" without form or personality? This is what the Old Church has taught, but what the New Church denies. We believe that the Deity is a being of infinite parts and affections, and that in His personality is contained the causative soul of every created thing; that in Him is something corresponding to everything that exists out of Him, and that nothing ever did or ever can exist apart from this correspondence.

This correspondence is of two kinds ; that of similarity and that of opposition. The first of these is directly of the Heavenly Father ; the second is indirectly of Him, because all power to will and to do is His ; but directly of the perversity of evil men and evil spirits. The first is of God's Providence, the second is of His permission.

All other creatures that God has made are without freedom. Their knowledge is instinctive ; and each one follows the bent of his own natural inclinations, without having any idea of right or wrong, of moral good or evil ; and therefore without having any responsibility. Man differs from all other creatures in being almost without instinct, and in being possessed of a freedom of thought and will that makes him capable of accepting or of rejecting whatever of good or evil is placed before him ; hence responsibility is one of his most marked and distinguishing characteristics. If he love the Lord and endeavor to keep His Commandments, true thoughts and good affections will fill his mind, and he will constantly grow to correspond more and more directly to his Heavenly Father. If he love himself and the world he will turn away from keeping the Commandments, and will grow constantly more in opposition to his Heavenly Father. The same faculty of loving which in the one is developed into a good affection, becomes in the other an evil passion. The same faculty of thinking which in the one is developed into forms of truth, in the other expands only into falsehood. The one is fostered by the Divine Providence because it is in harmony with the Divine Love and Wisdom; the other is permitted only that man may be left in perfect freedom.

The material world which surrounds us is designed to teach us what is within us; therefore we find in it all manner of good and evil things in animal, vegetable and mineral forms. All good and useful forms derive their existence directly from the Lord. All evil and noxious forms derive their existence directly from man, and indirectly from the Lord. The former are the outbirth and expression of the Divine Love and Wisdom. The latter are the result and expression of the evil and falsehood that is in man. The former by their beauty and usefulness are designed by the Providence of God to lead us in the path of

life. The latter by their ugliness and noxious-
ness are permitted by the same Providence,
that man may be repelled from the way of
death.

THE DAWNING DAY.

"The first watch of the morning is internal, pacific, and sweet, above the succeeding watches of the day." — SWEDENBORG.

I.

THE DAWNING DAY.

I FIND great pleasure, as well as instruction, in working in a garden. All the processes of gardening are full of suggestion to every mind that loves to think. The Lord is ever preaching to us in all His Providences; but in none of them more plainly than in the growth and development of the vegetable kingdom.

My garden is an open, sunny spot, lying in the midst of beautiful scenery. In front it is bounded by the village street; one of the prettiest that can anywhere be found; bordered on each side with luxuriant maple and ash trees, forming a long and beautiful avenue, such as would make a fitting approach to the finest house in the land; but which, to my mind, is all the more beautiful for belonging to everybody in the village, instead of being the property of a single individual. On the

opposite side of the way there stands a superb
grove of stately old elms, planted a century and
a half ago, to adorn the site of the parsonage,
which was built when the town was settled for the
second time, after having been totally destroyed
during King Philip's war. South of the garden,
separated from it by a small lawn, stands our old,
rambling house, whose age is more than a hun-
dred years, canopied by two immense elms, whose
youth no man remembers. On the west is a
deep, winding dell, shaded with a variety of fine
trees, and ending in a broad meadow, across
which, through the vista formed by the dell, the
eye wanders away northward, among groves of
walnuts and elms, and then to a village with its
heaven-pointing steeples, and distant, wooded hills
beyond.

In the warm summer mornings, I love to stand
in the midst of my garden and see the sun rise,
bathing the landscape with a refulgence of beauty
such as no other hour of his course ever bestows.
What the rosebud is to the rose, the early morning is to the rest of the day. There is a freshness
and purity in the aspect of the landscape then that
resembles nothing else so much as an opening
bud of the queen of flowers. There is a brilliant,

crystalline clearness in the atmosphere, too, that
gives a distinctness to the outlines of even distant
objects, which is never produced by the glaring
light of noon, nor the hazy gleam of the evening
twilight. It is Nature's most genial hour, when
her face glows with warmest welcome to her
lovers, unobscured by any of those veils of earthy
miasm that are sure to dim the lustre of her
beauty at a later hour.

I think I am right in believing that there is a
correspondence between this peculiar beauty of the
early morning and the commencement of the regenerate life. When the soul is first roused from
its stupor of worldliness and self-love, a door seems
suddenly to have opened through which we look
into the fair light of that city which has no need
of the sun, and we feel as if we should never
turn away from it to follow after the dim, earthly flame that has hitherto lighted our pathway. A vision of celestial beauty beckons us
to go with it into the New Jerusalem, and we
think we shall never tire, while our day of life
lasts, of strewing palm branches along the way
and singing psalms of joy and praise. This
period is of but short duration. The rising of
the natural sun soon causes the vapors of the

earth to ascend, and dim the transparency of the atmosphere, even in the fairest days; and so, in like manner, the spiritual sun shines in upon our souls, and as it rises higher and higher, reveals to us more and more of the noxious evils that permeate every fibre of our being. The warmer the sun shines the more quickly the vapors rise, and the more distinctly the evils of our nature become revealed to us. It may be that, as the day advances, we shall forget our vision of the morning, and, blinded by the mists that wrap us round, succumb to evil, until we lose our faith, so that our noon shall be shrouded in darkness, and our sun go down in the blackness of despair. Such cannot be the result of a genuine conversion. If the light and warmth of the early dawn awoke a sincerely answering love in the soul, the memory of that first vision of the heavenly life will go with us through every moment of the day, kindling a faith that shall give us light though thick clouds overshadow our path; giving us a rejoicing hope for brighter hours in store for us; and finally, burning with the steady flame of charity, shall keep the heart warm and the head clear in every trial and emergency life can bring.

The morning dawn is eloquent with life and

hope, and the promise of power to meet the toil that is to come. The evening twilight is suggestive of peaceful repose from the toil that is past. If the day of our life has been one of faithful effort, after the regeneration it will end in a twilight that shall say to the soul, "Depart in peace; for the morning that waits for thee shall know no diminution of its glories; but shall shine more and more brightly and clearly and peacefully throughout a perfect, eternal day."

FAITH WORK AND LOVE WORK.

"He who has love in his heart has spurs in his side."
PROVERB.

II.

FAITH WORK AND LOVE WORK.

I STINT myself to work an hour at weeding in my garden every morning before breakfast; but it often requires a good deal of effort to turn my eyes away from the beautiful landscape that surrounds me, and fix them upon the weeds at my feet; just as it is often very hard, and sometimes, to our wilful hearts, seems degrading, to turn from the study and contemplation of the sublimities of truth, and employ ourselves about the many little duties that go to make up the comfort of external life. As the success of the garden must depend on the care with which the weeds are removed, and the tender growth of the young plants watched over, so the comfort of the family depends on the performance of a thousand petty duties that go to make up the great sum of housekeeping.

A garden may be successful, and a house may be well kept; and yet the garden may be devoid of beauty, and the house may be an unhappy home. There is Mary's way and Martha's way of doing everything. Mary works from love, and Martha works from faith. Mary's heart works, and Martha's head works. Martha knows it is wrong to be idle; that in the sweat of the brow we are condemned to earn our bread; and she thinks that man was made for work. Mary, too, knows, when she stops to think about it, that it is wrong to be idle; but then she feels that it is pleasant to work; that the sweat of the brow brings no pain to those who work with love; that the body is more vigorous and the mind more elastic with those who work than with those who are idle; and she feels that work was made for man. With Martha work is an oppressive bondage, while with Mary it is an inspiring freedom.

The saying of the Lord to the Jews, who were enslaved by their ceremonial observances of the Sabbath, may be applied with equal propriety to many of our surroundings. Men and women are not made for the house, the garden, the farm, the profession; but all these are made for men and women. So long as we believe ourselves made

for duties we work like slaves ; but when we wake
to the truth that duties were made for us, we
come into the liberty wherewith the Lord makes
his children free. The soul grows in stature, and
beauty, and grace, by the doing of duty ; just as
the body grows in health, and strength, and skill,
by the exercise of its members.

The Marthas who seek the Lord sorrowing,
through wearisome and painful effort at doing
their duty as a hard task set before them, might
add warmth to their light, which is what they are
suffering for, if they would give more thought to
the exceeding love of God in making this world so
beautiful.   As I look around me, standing here in
the midst of my garden, it is evident to my mind
that God loves to work ; that creation is a delight
to Him ; and this is why He has made so vast
a variety of beautiful objects purely for the delight of the soul, and subserving no use to the
body.

I have seen more than one human being who
dared to walk through a flower-garden, with a
sneer upon the lip, and ask what use there was in
all this ; and it seemed to me that it was a profane
question, that could never have emanated from a
reverent heart.

It is very strange, and shows to what a low state man has sunk, that he calls only those things useful that subserve the life of the body; while those which feed and clothe the soul are called beautiful, but useless. Can a race of beings truly believe that they have souls and yet make such a distinction?

I am not one of those who think lightly of the body, or who overlook its wants; for I am well assured that every function of the body which works imperfectly is a fetter upon the movements of the soul; and therefore that we cannot be careless of the wants of the body without sinning against the soul. My garden is by no means a mere flower-garden. My endeavor is that it shall contain sufficient variety of fruits and vegetables, so that it may bring its tribute of comfort or luxury to the table every day in the year; but I think a garden that does not acknowledge the existence of a soul that loves the beautiful, by affording flowers as well as fruits, proves its owner deficient in the higher attributes of humanity. When it is evident that God loves flowers so much, since He adorns the earth with them so profusely, it is as evident that if we do

not love them we are so far not images and like-
nesses of the Creator.

Where we can count the varieties of plants that
are directly useful to the body by tens, we must
count those that are not so by thousands. If
these latter are of *no* use, we ask, like the un-
believing disciple, "To what purpose is all this
waste?" Here is material enough to make more
wheat, and potatoes, and rice, than would supply
the wants of the whole human race, wasted in
useless beauty; while thousands of men and women suffer for lack of food. It seems to me to
prove that God sets very little store by the body
compared with the soul, when he feeds the latter
so much more richly than the former.

Every creation from the hand of God must be
the expression of a Divine thought or feeling;
and if we study them reverently, and enjoy their
beauty with thankful hearts, our filial love for our
Heavenly Father must grow day by day, as we
learn more and more of the beauties and wonders
of His works. New plants are discovered every
year, by those who explore new countries, and
added to our gardens, to give us new varieties of
food, or to delight our sight and smell by their
beautiful forms and colors, or their delicious

odors; and men say, "How strange that these
plants should have grown for ages, wasting their
flowers and fruits to no purpose!" But does not
this wealth of creation teach us that God loves to
work; and that creation is the spontaneous out-
flowing of the Divine Life?

To Him in whose Infinite Thought a thousand
years are as one day, it must be but a small
matter that the flower blooms and fades, and the
fruit is perfected and decays, through a length of
time that to our finite thought seems immense.
He built the earth, and furnished it for man's
dwelling-place, and His love for man is such, that
it overflowed in the infinite variety of beautiful
forms that surround us; and this creative love did
not wait until man should be ready to take possession of each earthly mansion, but delighted
itself in preparing beforehand abodes for children
yet to come.

The slave who works from compulsion, and the
drudge who works merely for his hire, stop with
doing the least possible amount of work that they
can; but he who works from love, though it be
from a low and natural form of love, does a great
deal more than is required of him; while he whose
love is elevated and spiritual, works in true Chris-

tian liberty, seeking not his own, and loving his neighbor as himself; never inquiring what he *must* do, but striving to do all that he *can*.

Since human love works thus aboundingly, we can hardly be surprised to find the Divine Love, in whose image ours is formed, and from whose life ours derives its power, providing not merely for the support of life, but for its enjoyment, through every perception of both the spiritual and the natural body.

ELM SEEDS.

The seeming waste of nature is in fact a storing up of resources for future need; not a spendthrift loss of power.

III.

ELM SEEDS.

SO large a number of elms stand near by my garden that when the seeds ripen, let the wind blow from what quarter it may, it is sure to waft them within its limits, until its whole surface is thickly sown. They soon vegetate upon the loose earth, and after a few days it is difficult to find a square inch of soil that is not shaded by an infant tree. What a preparation is here for a forest! and yet all must be raked away and destroyed, that the growth of the garden plants may not be impeded. Of the seeds that fall in the neighboring fields and pastures, and by the roadside, where no one will notice them enough to destroy them, not one in a million will ever become a full grown tree. The very few that survive the accidents that will destroy most of them while young, will continue to make all the

region round about magnificent with their beauty
for centuries to come, as their parents are now
doing; but it seems strange that so much seed
should be wasted, when so small a quantity would
suffice to produce all the trees that will ever come
to maturity. Probably a single large tree produces in one year as many seeds as there will
be elms in the whole town for a million years.
Can this be the mere waste of the abounding
wealth of the Divine Creative Power? or is there
a meaning in it for our soul's instruction, and a
material use for the benefit of our bodies? A
little study and reflection will teach us that there
is food both for soul and body preparing in this,
as in every other, creation of the material world.

Vegetable growth and decay seem to have been
the means whereby the Creator has produced fertility over the whole earth. A little moisture on
the barren surface of a rock causes it to become
clothed with lichens; one of the lower forms of
vegetable growth. After a while these decay and
leave particles of soil upon the rock sufficient to
sustain the life of mosses, and these, passing away
in their turn, leave a little deeper coat of decayed
vegetable substance which suffices to support some
small, flower-bearing plant. Years roll on in this

way, until enough soil has been eliminated by suc-
cessive plants, acting upon the decaying rock, and
decaying in their turn, for a stately tree to find
abundant nourishment where once there was
nothing but hard, bare stone. This process goes
on slowly in our climate,—too slowly for a great
result to be observed by any one man; but in
tropical climates a very few years suffice to change
barrenness into fertility, whenever water, moisten-
ing mineral substances, causes the minute seeds
floating in the atmosphere to cling to them; and
they are afterward stimulated into growth by
heat and light. Desert sands, reefs of coral, fields
of lava, are transformed by these agents into fertile fields and stately forests. Geologists are led
to believe, by their investigations of the earth's
strata, that all vegetative soil was produced in this
way, by the gradual decay of mineral and vegetable substances. The plant devours the rock, and
the animal devours the plant. Thus the inorganic
substances of the earth become organized and fit
for the support of the material life of man. The
little elm seed, then, has not sprouted and expanded in vain, though I destroy it in the infancy
of its growth. Each one, by combining earth, air,
and water in its foliage, has organized a few grains

of inorganic matter; and its decay will help to enrich the garden for another year.

In the air we breathe infinitesimal seeds are constantly floating, imperceptible to any of our senses, but clinging to any damp surface, over which the air passes, and vegetating with wonderful rapidity into the curious growth that covers our food, our clothing, our books, with mould and mildew, unless we are watchful to guard against them by abundant ventilation. The use of this lowest form of vegetable life, which often becomes so troublesome and so offensive to man, seems to be to hasten the decay of all dead organic matter, thereby reducing it to a state in which it may subserve the use of a higher form of living, vegetable matter.

The Heavenly Husbandman is sowing seed, everywhere and at all times, without stint or measure; and covering the earth with vegetable growth faster than man can make use of it. So, too, He is sowing seed in our minds every moment of our lives. Every time that the senses take cognizance of sight or sound, of taste or smell or touch, a seed is sown; and every time a thought or feeling is aroused within us, a seed has germinated. These seeds spring up in our minds just as they do in the garden; bad and good, whole-some food and noxious poisons, fair flowers and unsightly weeds. There is, however, this differ-ence: The garden gives growth, without voluntary choice, to whatever germinates in its soil; but the mind of man, being endowed with free agency, gives growth only to what it loves. The Divine Gardener tends and nourishes the good seed that He plants in our minds, but He never pulls up the weeds that are planted there by the evil influences of the world. Just so fast as we pull up the weeds, He plants good seed in their places; but He does this only on condition that we first pull up the weeds. We begin to do this just as soon as we begin heartily to wish for good seed, and to feel our entire dependence upon Him for it. Love of the world and pride of character may induce us to pull up many weeds; but they are powerless to plant good seed. They only leave the ground swept and garnished, ready for weeds seven times worse than the first to spring up and overshadow the land with narcotic poisons that lull the soul into the sleep of death.

Some persons suppose that the human soul becomes regenerate by new and holy affections crowding out the old and unholy ones; but we

may as well hope to crowd the weeds out of our
gardens by planting roses and lilies among them,
as to rely on what Dr. Chalmers has called the
" expulsive power of new affections" to drive the
old leaven of unrighteousness from the heart.
The weeds must be torn up and cast away before
the good seed can find room to spread its roots
downward and its leaves upward.

They who strive to adopt virtues into their souls
without first having learned to hate their own
vices, and ceased to habituate themselves to them,
produce a result corresponding to the gardens that
may often be seen about the country, where the
seeds of good things are sown, and the roots of
fruit-bearing vines and trees are planted, but taken
no care of afterwards. They look as if there had
been days in the spring when the desire after good
things became active in the owner's mind; but the
true love of cultivation being wanting, the tall
weeds soon overtop and choke the growth of the
plants useful to man, while the couch-grass coat-
ing the surface, shows that its roots must form a
net-work everywhere beneath the soil, and by the
time the autumn comes will have taken possession
of the whole. One may gather a few currants
here and a handful of strawberries there, and per-

haps a fruit-tree may testify by a cluster of nice apples or pears what its whole growth would have borne had it been duly cared for; but the result of the whole is a melancholy failure, and a simple field of grass would have given the eye more pleasure and the mind more satisfaction.

This is no fanciful analogy; no idle invention of the imagination; but a true correspondence. Strive after virtue as we may, while our souls are still unconverted, hereditary evil is pervading our whole being, and constantly springing forth into sinful words and works; and though we may ever and anon check its external manifestations, it is still full of vitality within our hearts, like the couch-grass, whose roots traverse the under-soil of our gardens, ready to start above ground at every joint of their prolonged fibres, whenever the rain moistens them and the heat of the sun reaches them. The vices, too, that have been ingrafted upon us by external circumstances and associations, though not so deeply rooted, nor so intimately entwined in our natures, often spring into a more showy growth; like the tall rank weeds, which, though they have but little depth beneath the surface, spread a top so large as to overshadow the useful plants of more humble growth.

If we endeavor to plant new virtues in the soil where old vices are still growing we are striving to serve two masters; we are putting forth our hand to the plough and yet looking back; we are trying to take up the cross without denying self; and we have the assurance of the Divine Word that all such attempts are made in vain.

WEEDS.

"The noisome weeds, that without profit suck
The soil's fertility from wholesome flowers."

SHAKSPEARE.

IV.

WEEDS.

THE word weed has been defined in various ways. Some authorities give it the negative definition of "a plant out of place;" others give it the positive definition of "a useless or noxious herb." Since a weed corresponds to falses, the positive signification is the one which seems nearest the truth.

We sometimes say of a desirable plant that it grows, or spreads, like a weed; but the mind recognizes a difference between such and the true weed. So the exaggeration of virtues is sometimes perceived to run into something vicious; but still the mind acknowledges an essential difference between these, and vices that are so by their original constitution.

Since the Almighty is the Creator of all things, it becomes a question of interest why He created weeds ; and why He sows them so thickly over the earth.

In its broadest meaning, the earth and all that it contains corresponds to the races of men who people its surface. In a narrower sense it represents the individual man.

He who studies the natural sciences only in their relation to each other, or in order that he may find out how they can be made to minister to the material wants of man, stands only at the threshold of the great temple of nature. He is like one who reads the Bible and sees in it only an admirable book of laws, whereby men may be controlled and society harmoniously organized in this world ; but does not accept it as the veritable Word of God, spoken in order that men might become wise unto salvation. What the Bible teaches by language, the earth teaches by types and figures.

Weeds were not created, and do not grow so rankly, because they are in themselves good, although while they live they do their part in consuming the carbonic acid gas with which the atmosphere becomes loaded by the breath of animals, and in their decay by enriching the soil, even as the Psalmist tells us the wrath of man is overruled to praise the Lord, and its remainder restrained. They were created for our instruction, and are permitted to infest our cultivated ground to show us how false doctrines spring up in our hearts, and turn what should correspond to a well-tended garden into that which is represented by a tangled labyrinth of unsightly and useless or noxious weeds.

Those regions of the earth where man lives in a purely savage state, represent the human race destitute of the truths of religious faith, abounding here in natural goodness and there in natural wickedness, sometimes teeming with fertility and beauty, and sometimes barren and repulsive. In the more general meaning of this correspondence savage nations are typified; but it applies with equal truth and force to show us our own individual state before we awake to the necessity of regeneration.

Man, in the progress of civilization, becomes pastoral before he learns to be agricultural. To feed his flocks and herds he seeks for the natural pastures of the earth, where they may find grass, and uses some simple means for protecting and encouraging its growth. Grass, the most simple form of vegetable growth that is widely useful to

man, is the type of that goodness and truth which
come into life when man first begins to acknowledge his dependence upon the Heavenly Father,
and to desire to obey Him. It is the lowest form
of goodness and truth, such as reforms the external life, but does not bring the whole heart and
mind into willing obedience; for grass is not food
for man, but only for harmless brutes, such as are
made subservient to the wants of man. The soul is
planted only with grass when man lives in a state
of natural obedience to the laws of God, just as
the ox and the horse live in obedience to the hand
that feeds them, but without that free growth of
the affections which results in the entire bowing
down of the whole spiritual man before the throne
of the Heavenly Father, whom he worships with
the joyous freedom of perfect love. The higher
states of regenerate life are represented by corn,
the varieties of which are all grasses, but bearing
seeds which are fit for the use of man. Corn
growing in the fields is, like the grass of the pasture, the type of natural goodness, but of a much
higher order; because its seeds, by grinding and
baking, can be transformed into bread, or other
food for man, so nutritious and wholesome to the
body that it is the type which represents the celes-

tial goodness of the Lord, which nourishes and sustains the growth of the soul.

All wholesome fruits and seeds correspond to different forms of goodness and truth; for the soul requires variety of nutriment no less than the body, and the All-Beneficent Father creates want and supply with an even hand. Could man but be content with Eden,—could his soul crave only that which favors its heavenly growth, the instruction to be gained from weeds would have been unnecessary, and the trouble they occasion us would have been spared.

In order that man should be capable of goodness above that of the brutes, he must be created free; and he can be free to do good only so far as he is also free to do evil. As the forms of beauty and utility in the vegetable world illustrate, for our example, the virtues and graces of the soul, so its unsightly and noxious forms illustrate, for our warning, the vices and deformities that destroy the image and likeness of God in the spiritual body of man.

The tendency of the soil to produce weeds is commensurate with the enrichment bestowed upon it; just as the tendency to embrace false doctrines in the mind of man is commensurate with his intellectual cultivation. The Lord tells us that while we are blind we are free from sin, but when we say we see, our sin remaineth. Uncultivated tracts of country correspond to man ignorant of religious truth. Here the ground is not encumbered with weeds, and many wild flowers and fruits are produced, which are pleasant and beneficial to man. When something more and better is desired the turf is torn up by the plough-share, the natural flowers and fruits destroyed, and the seed of something esteemed more valuable is planted. The weeds are now sure to spring up side by side with the product of the good seed, and the struggle commences between nature and cultivation. Here is imaged the warfare of regeneration, and in the more or less careful cultivation of the field and the garden, which meets the eye as we traverse the country, each one of us may find the state of his own soul represented. While the turf remains unbroken in the pasture there is rest; but no sooner does the plough-share stir up the capacities of the soil than unceasing watchfulness and labor are called for. So there is quiet in the soul so long as that natural innocence of the mind continues which is the result of ignorance; but when truth breaks up this superficial virtue, and opens the soul to the influx of heavenly light, we begin to experience that the Son of Man came not to bring peace to the earth, but a sword. The war begins between good and evil, truth and falsehood. If we look forth upon our gardens we may learn much that will help us to understand the nature of this conflict; and in studying the success of the flowers and fruits of summer and autumn we may learn to comprehend many of the results brought about by the culture we bestow upon our own souls.

If we are careful to remove the weeds in the early part of the season, comparatively few spring up as the autumn approaches, and the offspring of the good seed finds, week by week, less opposition to contend with. Happy are those who work while it is spring-time in the garden of their souls; for vices that have been left to grow in the strong heat of the summer of life are very hard to up-root; and if we suffer them to abide till autumn we have little right to hope for anything but a winter of despair.

SQUIRRELS.

" I said of laughter, it is mad."
" There is a time to laugh."—SOLOMON.

V.

SQUIRRELS.

NTIL quite recently troops of the little striped squirrel have formed a pretty feature of my garden and its neighborhood. A large walnut tree near the house furnished them with their winter stores, and their merry gambols were a source of almost constant entertainment during the warmer months. Nothing could be more graceful than their mode of traversing the whole village, leaping from tree to tree with a rapidity and ease that seemed almost like the flight of a bird. No one, for a long time, thought of disturbing them, and they multiplied from year to year, and grew more familiar as they found nothing in the treatment they received to awaken their fears.

Nothing could seem more harmless than these happy little creatures; but, as their numbers in-

creased, it was found that they were so destructive
to the fruit of the pear tree that it became evident
we must make our choice between destroying the
squirrels or giving up this delicious fruit to their
enjoyment. A neighboring sportsman soon settled the question beyond debate ; and now, though
I miss the squirrels, I should not be willing to recall them at the price of the fruit. Their destruction of the pears was the more aggravating, because they ate nothing but the seeds. With their
sharp little teeth they would cut off the flower end
of the fruit, as if with a knife, just above the
seeds ; and, after picking these out, leave the stem
end hanging upon the tree. The quantity of fruit
they would destroy in a single day was quite as-
tonishing.

Another vexatious trick of these graceful little
animals, is their fondness for robbing birds' nests ;
devouring the eggs, or the recently-hatched birds,
with great avidity.

A few days since, as I was driving through a
retired wood, my attention was attracted by the
cries and alarmed excitement of two birds fluttering around the bough of a tree that overhung the
way. I stopped to ascertain what was the matter,
and soon found sufficient cause for the distress of

the poor birds in the person of a squirrel, who had ensconced himself in their nest, looking as much at home as if he were there of right.

The birds were of the smallest variety of sparrow, scarcely larger than humming-birds, and so much smaller than the squirrel, that their attacks, as they pounced upon him in their circling flights, seemed not to disturb his enjoyment in the least.

When I first caught sight of him he had an egg entirely within his jaws, which he could not quite close over it, so that I could see the shell all round his mouth between his teeth. He seemed to use a good deal of care in breaking the shell, as if he feared losing its contents, and then took one half of it out of his mouth with his right paw and tossed it from him, and then with the other paw removed the other half, with a jaunty sort of impertinence, as if he wished to show me he was quite at his ease out of my reach. For a few seconds he seemed to give himself up to the enjoyment of the delicate morsel, like a veritable epicure; then folding himself up, as if he intended passing the day in his stolen quarters, he put his head on one side, and fixed his keen little black eyes upon me, with an air that seemed to say, " And now, what do you propose doing about it?"

5

I watched him for some minutes; unable to reach him with any weapon I had at command, and then, finding he kept his position as if he never meant to stir, so long as I continued looking at him, I drove on, leaving the old birds still circling about him, and darting down upon him in vain efforts to drive him away.

It is difficult to restrain one's self from feelings of anger and resentment on seeing animals preying upon other animals; and yet it seems to be a law of the Divine Providence that each family of the animal races should be decimated to serve as food for some other family. Where any species is protected from such destruction it soon becomes so numerous as to be troublesome, and perhaps even injurious, although it may seem in its nature, like the squirrel, perfectly harmless and innocent. Restraint seems to be the first law of order in all created things. Without it everything impinges upon the liberty of its neighbor.

So, in the mind of man, no one trait, however innocent it may seem, can be indulged without restraint and not prevent the due development of other traits. Take for instance the playfulness of the mind, which seems to correspond to the gam-

bols of the squirrel. This is one of the most
pleasing attributes of childhood, and it is very desirable that it should be retained through life, for
it helps to lighten care and to keep the mind fresh
and buoyant. Still, this trait must, like every
other quality of the mind, be restrained, or it becomes positively vicious in its development, de-
generating into a levity that saps the foundation of
all those serious views of life which are absolutely
essential in the formation of a character of any
moral worth.

Levity is often an amusing trait, and when accompanied by grace and beauty has sometimes a
fascinating power, when one is unconscious of,
or indifferent to, its dangerous tendencies. Pleasing persons, in whom levity is a dominant vice, are
often excused for the faults, and even the sins, into
which it betrays them; because, as their apologists
say, " they are so good-hearted." The phrase
" good-hearted," when used in this manner, means
only that the individual has a pleasant way of giving an amusing or impertinent reason for his
wrong doing; and it implies nothing of that goodness of heart which finds its life in love to the
Lord and to the neighbor.

Playfulness that degenerates into levity is the offspring of vanity and irreverence, and contains no element of goodness. There is no more hopeless state of the mind than when it finds pleasure in sporting with what others deem sacred, and laughing at things morally wrong.

The sportiveness of the human mind that expresses itself in laughter is something entirely peculiar to the human race. The brute creation demonstrate their joy by various bodily movements, but no one of them has the power of laughter. The reason of this is, that laughter is the expression of a certain kind of intellectual pleasure. Other animals are purely affectional, while man is intellectual beside being affectional. All animals display the delight of their affections by various movements of the body, and man by smiles; but laughter is the result of intellectual satisfaction at some novelty of thought.

Laughter is of two distinct kinds. The one is the result of sympathy, the other of antagonism. The one laughs *with* its object, the other laughs *at* it. The one partakes of the character of its object, and may be either good or evil. The other always despises its object, and is, by its own nature, necessarily evil. We laugh *with* the ludicrous; we laugh *at* the ridiculous.

The wisest of Jewish kings tells us in one place that laughter is madness, and in another that there is a time to laugh. When we hear the free, ringing, innocent laughter of childhood, we can feel that there is a time to laugh. When we hear the depreciating, the triumphant, or the bitter laugh of manhood, we can understand that it is madness.

The mode in which a person laughs is a very sure index of the character. The laugh of early childhood is free from sin as the song of birds, or the gambols of beasts. The whole being is so single that the gayety of the soul dances forth into the movements of the body, and the joyousness of the affections vibrates along the vocal organization with impulses too interior to be formed into words, and so they express themselves in laughter. There is, perhaps, no purer emotion excited in the adult mind than that which we feel when listening to the happy laughter of childhood. It carries us back to our own early life, and renews within our soul glimpses of the time when our angels continually beheld the face of the Heavenly Father.

This sweet, childish laughter is rarely retained through life. As fast as evil passions are aroused in the mind, so fast the character of the laughter changes. There is the loud, empty laugh " that speaks the vacant mind ; " the tittering of silliness ; the coarse laugh of vulgarity ; the scornful laugh of the cynic ; the bitter laugh of the misanthrope ; the sardonic laugh of the hypocrite ; the exulting laugh that rejoices in the inferiority of its subject ; the refined, intellectual laugh, which delights in subtle distinctions and acute witticisms ; and in the depraved, who seldom laugh heartily, there is the " depreciating sneer," at which the painter Allston used to say he thought the devil must laugh more heartily than at anything else.

The laughter of childhood is almost purely affectional, and has its life in the same influx from heaven that, descending into the lower animals, produces gambols and songs. As childhood ceases, if its purity remain, this same affection displays itself in a happy, smiling countenance, that seems radiant with inward joy. There is nothing in it that ever suggests the idea of superciliousness or self-complacency. The kindly old age that follows tells every year more and more of purity, and gentleness, and love, and peace. It is full of Christian charity, and, though laughing seldom, in its laughter it is always sympathetic. It laughs only *with* innocently ludicrous things that invite laughter; while ridiculous things *at* which others laugh give it only pain.

BIRDS AND OTHER THINGS.

Analogy sometimes carries a clearer conviction to the mind than argument.

VI

BIRDS AND OTHER THINGS.

ALKING lately along the border of the intervale that stretches away for two or three miles to the North of my garden, I observed a pair of red-winged black-birds flying near me. I suppose I had approached their nest, from the manner in which they flew around me in rather a wide circle; but keeping sufficiently near to show that I was an object of suspicion to them. Sometimes their flight was rapid, with a quick fluttering of the wings; then they would close the wings entirely, and dart a considerable distance through the air, descending a little, and looking more like a fish than a bird. When they were preparing to alight, they floated downward with a movement so graceful, and withal so gentle, that it could be compared to nothing but that of a wreath of smoke. They almost always chose some slender weed for

their alighting place, which one would have supposed too feeble to sustain them, but which swayed
so slightly under their weight that it seemed as if
there were some secret sympathy between the
plant and the bird, by which the one became
strong to bear, while the other became light to
be borne.

The way in which the crimson feathers of the
outer side of the wing came into view and then
disappeared again, as the birds circled around me,
was very beautiful.   Sometimes only the jetty
black of the under parts of their little forms could
be seen.   Then a sudden turn in their flight would
bring the crimson feathers flashing in the sun, and
make them gaudy as butterflies.

While I stood watching them, a crow came in
sight, and sailed heavily over the meadow, pur-
sued by a little bird who, having mounted into a
higher region of the air, and being much quicker
in its movements than the crow, was able to torment him by darting down and striking his back
with its bill, in a way that evidently tormented the
great, clumsy bird; but from which he seemed
quite unable to escape.

The grace and elegance of the black-birds, the
ponderous weight of the crow, and the agile

combativeness of the little bird, thus brought into direct contrast, offered an interesting illustration of some of the doctrines of correspondences, as they have been given us through Swedenborg.

All winged animals correspond to thoughts, true or false, wise or foolish, pacific or combative, pure or unclean.

Endlessly varied as are the tribes of insects and of birds, even so varied are the thoughts that throng the brain of man. The old Greeks, when they called man a microcosm or little universe, comparing him with the macrocosm or great universe, uttered a literal and precise truth. It is probable that this truth was handed down orally from the most ancient Church that dwelt in Eden, and the wise Greeks could see, in a general way, that it was a truth. In the light of the New Church we are enabled to perceive this truth with a particularity to which the Greeks could not have attained, and which fills the natural sciences with a life and interest hitherto unknown.

To know ourselves is of the utmost importance, in order that we may be able rightly to cultivate ourselves; and for this reason the world around us was created a vast mirror, in which our thoughts and affections, which constitute the all of our humanity, are reflected.

The love and the wisdom of the Heavenly Father, coming down into the world of matter, are shaped by His power into the various orders of existence. Every mineral, every vegetable, and every animal creation, if it be innocent, is the expression of some Divine affection or thought. On these Jehovah looks and declares them good. These are created to lead us upward toward Him, by showing us the beauty of the Divine order. These are the music of the universe, attuned into heavenly harmonies; and we harmonize with them when we love the Lord with the whole heart, and, because we so love Him, love the neighbor as ourselves.

But there are discords as well as harmonies in the universe; things noxious as well as beneficent; fearful as well as lovely. These too exist from the power of God, but by His permission, not by His approval. In them are mirrored the traits of man's soul, distorted by love of self and love of the world. Passions like wild beasts, that hide themselves from the light of day in dens of falsehood, to prowl secretly in darkness and destroy the neighbor. Lusts that crawl like _ _les upon the earth, defiling it with their touch. Thoughts that soar with strong wing, as if to scale the heavens, but in reality only the better to scan the earth for living prey, or, baser yet, for carrion. Fantasies soaring in clouds like locusts, obscuring the light of the heavenly sun, and then falling upon every green thing that sun vivifies, leaving nothing in their track but desolation and famine.

Man's spiritual nature is not yet sufficiently educated to enable him to comprehend his own soul, so as to perceive all the correspondences that have relation to it in the world around him. Enough may however be learned to be of great use to him in self-analysis, and the capacity for learning increases wonderfully by use. Every time we make a direct personal application to ourselves of what we have already learned, we cast out some portion of that blinding beam of self-love which makes it so hard for us to perceive the truth; for it is not abstractly studying the truth, but doing it, that gives us the ability to know the doctrines.

Whatever we see around us has its correspondence within us, either in the natural or the spiritual part of our being. As we contemplate the

external objects of nature we should not stop when
we have admired or condemned, when we have
experienced either delight or disgust. In all our
observations we should bear in mind that what we
contemplate is the type of something within ourselves; that everything we see corresponds to and
illustrates some active principle, or some latent
capacity, either good or evil, within our own souls.
When we contemplate things evil or noxious, if
we do not remember that we have a capacity for a
corresponding evil in our own nature, our self-
esteem is stimulated, and we gain only harm from
what we see; but if we keep this truth in mind
our humility is awakened, and we are put upon
our guard against giving way to the impulses of
our lower nature. So in observing things good,
if we are not awake to the truth that here is something for our imitation, something to guide us in
the formation of our own souls, we gain no more
to our spiritual being than we should gain to our
natural bodies if we took food into our mouths
and then neglected to swallow it.

The same truth holds good in our observations
of our fellow beings. If we study human nature
in the neighbor, unmindful of our common humanity, all that we see of evil makes us censorious

or self-complacent; and we constantly grow more fond of finding out and condemning evil in those around us, forgetting that as we judge, even so shall we be judged. When, on the contrary, we remember our common brotherhood, we see the vices of the neighbor with pain; and feeling our own liability to fall in the same way, we judge him compassionately, and are put upon our guard against falling into a similar vice in our own persons. In the one case we are learning to hate the neighbor, in the other to love him. In the one case we are cultivating hardness of heart, in the other we are learning to be perfect after the manner in which the Heavenly Father is perfect.

THE SOWING OF SEED.

"Sow with a generous hand,
  Pause not for toil or pain,
  Weary not through the heat of summer,
  Weary not through the cold spring rain,
  But wait till the autumn cometh,
  For the sheaves of golden grain."

VII.

THE SOWING OF SEED.

THERE is no garden process more instructive than the sowing of seed. Sow it carefully as we may, it often comes to naught, for several circumstances must combine to make it spring up and grow. In the first place it must be good seed, then it must not be sown carelessly on the surface of the earth, nor buried too deeply below the surface. Then the soil must be appropriate to the kind of seed we sow, and it must be well dug up, and prepared to nourish the little plant when it begins to grow. All these preliminaries being attended to, we still are not sure of the result, because that, finally, depends on the descent of a due proportion of sunshine and of rain, over which we have no control. Though we do all that we know how to do, we still work in ignorance of the final result of our efforts. Should

(85)

this discourage us, or make us less willing to sow our seeds? Surely not; for though we may be many times disappointed, we are also sure of many times succeeding. Only let us be patient, and remember that Providence is over all, the least as well as the greatest, of the efforts of our lives. In the garden, as everywhere else, we learn that there is a power above us that controls all things; and our disappointments, when we do all that it is in our power to do to insure success, never come any oftener than we need them to check the pride and presumption of our self-love. Results are in the hand of Infinite Love and Infinite Wisdom, and are measured out in perfect adaptation to the needs of each individual. Happy are we if we accept the lesson that each success and each disappointment is designed to teach. Happy are we if, though we may be unable to comprehend the lesson, we use our success as a talent entrusted to us by our Heavenly Father, or bow before our disappointment in humble faith that He withholds success because we are not in a state to be benefited by it.

Our whole lives are a continual sowing of seed; for not only every thing we say and do, but even our silence and indolence, are seeds which, sooner or later, will produce each its appropriate harvest. We scatter words carelessly around us as if nothing were to come of them ; but they are ever liable to find a place where they may take root in the mind of some person who hears them, and we should beware that the seed we thus sow is such that good fruit may be its result. If thistles are suffered to grow in our own garden, the seeds will surely blow over and take root in some garden near us ; and just so will the idle words that overflow from our evil passions cling in the mind of some neighbor, and bring forth fruit to our shame.

Our example, too, sows seeds more deeply and effectually than our words, and this should make us doubly careful what we do. In a careless and unthrifty neighborhood, if one individual puts his own place in order, an example and a stimulus are given to others, and in a little while the aspect of the whole village will be changed to neatness and order. In like manner the example of a truly devout and virtuous life is a blessing that we cannot measure to all who come within its influence. There is no exhortation so eloquent, no reasoning so unanswerable. We must not, however, think too much of sowing the gardens around us ; for in that case we shall be liable to neglect our own, and it is there our first duty lies. No amount of care for the interest of the neighborhood will compensate for unfaithfulness at home. If we pluck up the noxious weeds at home before the seeds ripen, we shall be sure of doing no injury to the neighbor by planting evil seed in his ground, and we shall make space for the growth of good and beautiful plants in our garden that may furnish seed for others by and by. Only let us be careful to retain seed enough for our own ground. We may think so much of giving the truth to others that we forget to make any application of it to ourselves, thereby making our gift of no avail; for preaching has little or no effect unless enforced and illustrated by a life in accordance with its precepts.

When a child first begins gardening, he is so impatient to see the result of his work that he is almost sure to dig up his seeds in order to find if they are sprouting. The parent looks on and perhaps smiles complacently at the child's folly, bidding him be patient for a few days till the little plants have time to show themselves. Yet it is quite probable that that very parent treats the seeds of thought he sows in the mind of the child with an impatience just as foolish as that of the

child over his flower-seeds. He tells him a truth
and expects it to spring up and bear fruit as soon
as it is sown. He looks to reap the harvest in the
character of his child before the seed time is over.
He probes his child's heart with questions to find
out if the truth he sows is germinating before the
warmth of the Divine Love has had opportunity
to expand the germ and quicken it into life. He
will not wait for the gradual way in which the
Divine Providence, through the ministry of circumstance, quickens the spiritual nature of the
child; and then by the rain of His truth and the
sunshine of His love causes the seeds sown, it
may be years before, and lying till then darkly and
inertly, to take root and grow, and bear fruit
manyfold.

Seeds have many ways of springing. Some of
them come up almost immediately, and in a few
weeks are covered with bloom. Others come up,
but remain of little worth during the first year of
their life, blooming only the second. Others again
require long terms of years to bring the time of
the blossom and the fruit; and it is the plants of
the greatest value that, for the most part, require
the longest time to arrive at perfection. In one
point they all agree. Before there is any growth

upward into the light and air, there is always a growth downward, in darkness and secrecy. The delicate rootlets must first clasp the earth, and be prepared to draw nourishment from it, before the tender blade begins to grow. All this corresponds precisely with the growth of the principles of truth in the human mind; and all this should teach us to sow patiently, and wait the Lord's good time for the springing of the seed and the whitening of the harvest. Our touch is too rude to permit our opening the ground with safety; and we must content ourselves with letting the seed go through the first stages of growth in the secret places of the soul, that can be penetrated only by the eye of Omniscience.

In like manner we must be patient with ourselves. We understand little, if anything, more of the growth of truth inward in our own souls than in the souls of neighbors; but this inward growth must, nevertheless, take place before there can be any outward sign. We cannot tell whence or how the Holy Spirit breathes the breath of life into the soul. There are times when we feel as if we were making no progress. Our minds seem so dead that nothing can grow there, just as the earth lies in our gardens when long, cold rains come after seed-sowing. We must wait and watch, sustained by faith that the sun is behind the clouds, and will after a while prevail over them. Meanwhile we must not let the weeds grow and choke the ground, for then there will not be room enough for the good plants. It is not the will of the Divine Gardener that any of His seed should perish; and it will not, if we keep the ground clear of weeds, and softened by cultivation, so that the warmth of the sun may penetrate it, and the little roots may be able to find their way between its particles. In other words we must resist all temptation to do evil, and must strive to live in charity with those around us. Just so far as the heart is shut up with selfishness and with indifference to the happiness of those around us, it is hardened against receiving the influences of the Divine Love; while every kind thought and word and deed that warms the heart towards the neighbor prepares it to receive the life-giving influx that comes down to us from Him who has said, " Inas much as ye have done it to the least of these ye have done it unto me."

Probably every person who has reached mature life has experienced the sudden and unexpected quickening of truths that had long lain inert in the mind, and almost forgotten. The being placed in new circumstances, bringing out new wants or capacities in the mind, or setting in motion new trains of thought, will often recall some text of Scripture, or some wise saying of man, which we long since heard or read without giving any special heed to it, but which now rises in the memory and suddenly expands into a growth of beauty and of power that fills us with surprise and delight.

In the tribulations and bereavements of life, when the heart is bowed down and bruised and torn in every fibre, so that it seems impossible its wounds can ever heal, after days and weeks, perhaps months of despair, all at once, we know not how or why, some phrase of consolation will rise in the memory like a strain of soft music, and subdue us into listening silence, as the stormy waves sank into quietness at the " Peace! Be still!" of the Lord. We had, perhaps, known the words from our childhood, but they had never been of any personal interest to us before. We had not thought of them, it may be, for years. Now they come to us with a tender pleading that cannot be resisted, and suggest new trains of thought, and open new sources of emotion, and there is a great calm in the tempest wherein we had been struggling so long. We are lost in wonder at what manner of power this is that has suddenly taken possession of us and subdued us to His own paternal will, till our anguish and our want of submission are lost in the enfolding arms of eternal love. The little seed, so small we had never before given it a thought, has grown into a great tree, overshadowing our whole being.

One such experience in a life should suffice to teach us the lesson of sowing seed in faith, and waiting for its upspringing in patient hope and loving charity. One such life experience is better than anything the garden can tell us; but still it is pleasant to see how the natural ever illustrates the spiritual, and a new interest is given to the processes of nature when we observe how they correspond with the workings of the spirit.

Some years since I planted a handful of the red seed-vessels of the sweet-brier, without being aware how slowly they germinate. I looked for them all through the summer in vain, and supposed they had perished in the ground. The next season the earth was dug up without any regard to them, and other flowers were planted over them that grew and blossomed more readily, but no sign came from the briers. The third year I was care-

lessly weeding the spot, not supposing anything
of worth was there, when I perceived the peculiar
odor of the sweet-brier. I was puzzled for a moment whence it could come, as there were no plants
of it in the garden that I knew of. Then I re-
membered that here was the spot where I had so
long since planted the seeds, and on carefully separating the weeds I found ten little briers, which,
though scarce an inch in height, filled the air all
around them with delicious fragrance. They have
grown and flourished since into tall and graceful
plants, and as I look upon them they preach me
this sermon.

When you sow precious seed, have faith that it
will, under the Heavenly Father's Providence, some
day spring into life; and in the name of Him who
has said, I will not break the bruised reed, nor
quench the smoking flax, I conjure you beware
that in rudely plucking up weeds you do not destroy the infant germs of immortal and heavenly
life. Not only must you sow your seeds with
care, but you must also be tender of the little
plants. Silence your impatience when it tells you
that the seeds of truth have died in the mind of
him whom you would influence; neither be too
eager in your endeavors to weed out the vices that

may obstruct their growth. By too impatient or rude a handling you may kill or discourage his virtues. In plucking the mote from his eye, if your touch be not delicate you will, at the same time, quench his sight.

ABOUT SEEDS.

The seed with its germ and its albumen, the cause and the end of all vegetable life, is the type of the Divine Wisdom with its truth and its goodness, the cause and the end of all spiritual life.

VIII.

ABOUT SEEDS.

THE seed is the beginning and the end of all plants. From it the plant springs, and to produce it the whole plant tends. When a plant has gone to seed, it has completed a cycle of existence. With many plants there is but one such cycle. The seed being perfected, the plant withers away, its whole use performed. Other plants produce seed year after year; but still the producing of the seed is the crowning act of their lives; the completion of a cycle.

The seed is composed of two parts; the germ, and the albumen, which is the food on which the germ is to live during the first stage of its growth. The development of the germ requires moisture, warmth, and air, in order that the albumen may be softened so that it can be absorbed by the germ, and in order to quicken the germ so that it may be

in a state to absorb the food prepared for it. Light
impedes, and sometimes even prevents germina-
tion, by producing a chemical change in the albumen that renders it unfit for nourishing the germ.
The germ is the *form* of life in the seed, the albumen its *essence*. Either separated from the other
cannot live and grow. The germ is as it were the
body, and the albumen the soul of the seed.

The germs of seeds are so small that they have
very little value as food for man ; but the albumen
forms a very large proportion of the food of the
human race. In all the cereal grains, in rice, and
all the seeds and nuts that man uses for food, it is
the albumen that nourishes his life. The albumen
that is created expressly as food for germs, becomes also the bread of life for the material body
of man.

Man has two bodies, the one material, the other
spiritual. He does not live by bread alone, but
by every word that proceedeth out of the mouth
of God. Precisely as bread sustains his material
life, so the Word of God sustains his spiritual
life.

Truth, as it comes from God, is never separated
from goodness. Truth is the germ in the seed
that God sows, and it is always sustained and

nourished by the albumen of goodness. Every Divine truth is a germ that grows because it is a form adapted to receive the inflowing life of goodness. If a truth lies in the mind without any appropriate accompanying goodness, it dies there as surely as a seed dies in the ground if the albumen is separated from the germ.

It is one of the besetting sins of man to desire to separate truth from goodness; to strive after salvation by faith alone. The belief in the saving power of faith is not confined to the sects that hold it as a dogma, but is one of the most common traits in the mind of man. He is ever fancying that he shall finally be saved by the good thoughts he entertains, though his life may be far from exemplifying them.

We read the life of some admirable man, or the story of some noble deed, or we hear preached a delineation of some exalted virtue, and our enthusiasm is excited, and we fancy that we possess in ourselves capacities for the virtues we admire; and that opportunity alone is wanting to enable us to exemplify them in our own lives. We feel so good as we read or listen, that we are quite sure we must be quite as good as we feel. Others may deny the Lord, but we never can. Within

the hour, as it were before the cock crows, the
opportunity is given us to do something requiring
but a tithe of the sacrifice or the effort we have
been admiring, and we refuse to do it. We are
told perhaps a second and a third time that it is
our duty, but we deny it; we know nothing of
this man whom we are supposed to follow and to
serve. If there is a genuine love of goodness in
our hearts, founded upon an acknowledgment of
the Lord as the only source of true goodness,
the cock will crow before we have done with the
matter; and we shall, like Peter, acknowledge
our sin with repentant tears. If, on the contrary, we love goodness only because the abstract
contemplation of it makes us feel happy by exciting a self-complacent idea that we also are
good, we are aiming at salvation by faith alone,
and there is no true love of goodness in us. We
are separating the ideal from the real, the true
from the good, faith from works. Our spiritual
nature does not live by the undivided words of
God. We are separating the parts of the Divine
seed that is given for our nutriment, and our
spiritual bodies can never be developed into the
image and likeness of the Divine Being, who
created us with capacities by means of which we

might attain to heavenly happiness, by resembling Him.

In turning from the temptation to believe in salvation by faith alone, we are liable to fall into the opposite one of believing in salvation by works alone. This belief often results in a life of great external purity, but it is very sure to engender a pride and self-complacency that is quite foreign to that denial of self which the Lord so constantly inculcates. This has been carried to such an extent that it is not uncommon to hear pride spoken of as a virtue. The phrases, proper pride, becoming pride, and even virtuous pride, are used by many with apparent unconsciousness that there is anything in them opposed to the words of Christ; but if we exalt pride among the virtues, how are we to dispose of the inculcations to humility, meekness, and self-denial with which the gospels abound. To deny self is the first requirement the Lord makes of us; the initial step into the Christian life; while pride is the very opposite of this, and so entirely incompatible with it that both cannot exist in the same mind, excepting in a state of warfare which must result in the triumph of one and the destruction of the other;

whenever the mind becomes established either in good or evil, as every mind eventually must.

When we believe in salvation by works alone, we reject the germ from the seed the Heavenly Gardener plants in our minds, and so the truth ceases to grow within us. We soon get to think that it is of no consequence what we believe, or whether we believe anything; and while our faith in God grows daily weaker, our faith in self as constantly grows stronger; and the end is that we worship self instead of God.

Whether we reject the germ or the albumen from the heavenly seed, the result is alike fatal to Christian growth; for that demands of us to accept the whole truth, undivided, as it comes down from heaven. We must love the Lord supremely, and believe in Him as the only source of goodness and truth; and looking to Him as the fountain whence we draw all knowledge of what is true, and all power to do that which we know, we must be perfect in our daily lives after the manner in which our Heavenly Father is perfect. Then we shall be free from the bigotry that results from believing in salvation by faith alone, and from the pride of life that results from believing in salvation by works alone; for neither of these vices can exist in a mind that worships the Lord in humility, and loves the neighbor as itself.

If our minds have proved a grateful soil for the reception of heavenly seed, we shall desire to scatter it in turn for the benefit of others. To do this wisely, we should remember that if we give the bare, hard truth, it is only a germ we have sowed, and we have no right to expect that it will grow. Our thoughts must be enfolded in our affections, and nourished by them, before they can expand, and shape themselves into a Christian life, and before they can utter themselves in words that will express the truth as it comes down to us from the Lord. Love is the albumen that nourishes truth. If we would teach our neighbor we must love him, and we must love the truth. We must love the truth because it is the Word of God, and therefore infinitely perfect; and we must love the neighbor because he is one of God's children, and we owe to him every act of spiritual kindness that he will receive from us.

The Lord describes the Heavenly Gardener sowing seed in all soils, and we must imitate Him. We cannot be sure of the adaptations of the soils in which we sow material seed, for there are secret

powers in the earth which the chemist has vainly
sought-to understand, which prevent us from being able to decide positively, beforehand, whether
it is adapted. to the kind of seed we wish to sow.
Far more difficult is it for us to decide upon the
capacities of the spiritual soils we would cultivate,
and we shall often be surprised by a rich harvest
where we sowed with little hope, and disappointed
by failure where we anticipated success.

The same traits of character that prepare us for
receiving heavenly seed to advantage qualify us
for giving it to others. Humility in receiving, and
patience in well-doing, give us the power of be-
stowing what we receive in a way that will make
it acceptable to those to whom we give it. What
we receive humbly we give in the same way; for
we hold it and give it as something that is not
ours, but the Lord's. When we acquire a truth
and hold it as if it were our own, our pride is
inflated; and then, if we try to teach it to another,
we do it in such a way that we excite his pride in
opposition to ours, and cause him to close his
mind against us. It was *our* truth we were trying
to give him, and not the Lord's; therefore the
Lord could not help us to give it, and we were
left with no sustaining impulse but that which

comes from the demon of Pride. The sun and the rain of heaven could not reach and soften the albumen of such seed, and the germ was dried up and destroyed by the fire of earthly passion.

When we find ourselves angry because people do not take the truth we offer, we may be sure that we are not offering them the truth as it is in Jesus. We may have the form of truth, but we have not its spirit; and we should turn at once and examine our own hearts, and convert ourselves before we undertake the conversion of others. We can give only after the same manner that we receive. If we receive in the love of self we shall give in the love of self, and have small reward for what we do. If we receive in love to the Lord, we shall give in the Lord's name, and much fruit will be the result.

Patience in well-doing is the trait second in importance in qualifying us to sow seed rightly; because if we work patiently in cultivating our own souls we shall appreciate the troubles and difficulties that obstruct the progress of others, and we shall learn to wait patiently for their growth in grace.

There is great danger of saying too much when we would instruct, especially to children. The

truth is very simple, and does not need to be en-
larged upon elaborately in order to make it manifest. We are more apt to obscure it than to
make it plain by many words. Having spoken
it, let it be, quietly; and do not repeat day after
day the same thing. It is not good to overseed
ground, for thereby all growth is choked. Remember, too, that seeds cannot sprout well in the
light; and, therefore, refrain from trying to look
in upon the early stages of mental growth in your
child or your friend. The influence of your affection going forth constantly in kind words and
deeds, will keep the truths you give warm and
soft, like the sunshine and rain of heaven, and
they will probably germinate in good time; but if
they do not, your much talking and watching
would have done no more good than it would to
keep stirring up the soil in your garden in order
to quicken the sprouting of the seeds you plant
there.

It is probably overseeding of the mind that
causes the children of pious but over-anxious
parents often to grow up with no religion at all.
Too much preaching is as bad for the soul, as too
much seed for the soil. No fruitful growth will
come of it.

Plant and water as we may, it is God who giveth the increase. We should endeavor to be sure that we sow good seed, and that we sow it with a loving spirit. Having done that, we should not try to compel its growth by perpetually working over the soil, nor sow too soon again, nor at an inappropriate season, in our eagerness to produce a harvest.

THE CHANGING SEASONS.

Change is the renewing of all things. An atmosphere without motion, an ocean without tide, will not more certainly breed miasma and death to the body than will unchanging circumstance bring stupor and destruction to the soul.

IX.

THE CHANGING SEASONS.

AUTUMN has laid its hand heavily upon my garden, and all that remains to be done there now is to prepare for winter. There is much that is desolate both in Spring and Autumn; but there is a great contrast between the desolation that precedes the winter and that which follows it. Autumn is in itself very beautiful; far more so than the Spring; but the natural tendency of the mind is to mourn in the fall of the leaf, and to rejoice in its putting forth. Still no season is truly mournful. Each has its appropriate enjoyments; and there is enough to enjoy in each to fill the devout heart with thanksgiving.

We are prone to criticise and condemn things as well as persons for what they are not, instead of valuing them for what they are. We dwell upon their deficiencies instead of their qualifications. If we compare Spring and Autumn in relation to what they really possess of positive beauty, Autumn has a very great superiority; and yet most persons call the Spring the most beautiful, because then their own imaginations are filled with the anticipation of the beauty of Summer; while in Autumn they are blinded to the present beauty by the wintry images filling the perspective that stretches away before the mind's eye.

In the Spring nothing is left but the bare forms of hills and valleys, of forests and scattered trees, brown and desolate; while harsh winds and cold rains continually check and disappoint our hopes. "Winter lingering in the lap of Spring," allows us few days of genial warmth until Summer has almost come; yet we constantly comfort ourselves under our disappointments with the hope that Summer must come. Until almost the very last of the Spring we have nothing of beauty in color to gratify the eye as it wanders over the landscape, and almost nothing of warmth to console the touch; but we feed on hope day by day, and so endow the Spring-time with a beauty not its own. Compare the best day that Spring can give us with any fine Autumn day, and how poor it seems!

The scattering days, and now and then a week of
what is called the Indian Summer, are unsurpass-
able for beauty in the whole circle of the year.
The air is dry and soft and warm, and the landscape glowing with purple and crimson and gold.
As I walk through my garden now, if I am
saddened by the black and withered plants that
surround me, I have but to lift my eyes to the
hills, and I am helped. The trees near by have
most of them cast their leaves; but their shade,
that was so grateful in summer, is no longer
wanted; and the neighborhood being now less
embowered, the eye can wander at will over the
graceful outlines of the hills that encircle the
view, clothed in robes that seem beautiful enough
for curtains to paradise. Crimson oaks, and rich
evergreens, and yellow chestnuts, mingle their
hues, and golden vistas between the hills invite
the eye to look for something even more beautiful
beyond, like gateways leading into a celestial city.
A fair, high, round hill lies to the westward,
crowned with a wood of chestnuts, all clad in
yellow of the softest and richest tint, their rounded
tops looking like curled, soft wool; suggesting to
my fancy a golden fleece spread out in the sunshine. Jason could hardly have needed a vision

more beautiful to lure him onward in his adventurous search.

For all that affords perfect sensuous delight, I know of nothing in the whole circle of the year that equals the fine days of Autumn. Genial warmth to the touch, exquisite beauty to the eye, and for the ear that almost supernatural stillness that suggests rest after toil, peace after struggle. It is the Sabbath of the year. The labor of the seed-time and the harvest is past, and now is the season for quiet thought, for counting up our possessions, and seeing what we have gathered that will sustain us through the winter that is soon to come.

The four seasons are, like all of life, just what we choose to make of them. If we accept them as gifts from the hand of the Heavenly Father, they are all rich in bounty. If we look at them without reference to the Divine Hand, they will all receive the shadow of our ingratitude, and reflect to our minds the discontent we carry to them.

The seasons correspond to the different periods of the life of man. Youth, with its little of attainment and its much of hope; mid-life, with its fulness of vigor, bodily and mental; full age,

when the bodily powers become less active, and
the mind more given to contemplation; and old
age, when that which we have actually attained
through all the preceding seasons is made manifest; and the poverty or wealth of the character
we have been building up is displayed in gloomy
discontent at the remembrance of the things of
this world which we are losing, or in peaceful
happiness at the anticipation of the world we are
soon to enter.

The seasons also correspond to the progressive
states through which we pass in the different periods of the mind's development. The inner life
is counted by years as well as the outer,—spiritual years, having all the varied phases of the
changing seasons in the natural year. The mind
has its spring-times of hope, when some new truth
is germinating within it, and filling it with visions
of heavenly uses that are to result from it in the
daily life; — its summers of joy, as these uses
develop in kind words and loving deeds; — its
autumns of contemplation, when the soul, having
completed a cycle of progress, and gathered from
it all the fruits that it can harvest, passes into a
winter of sadness and desolation, through fear that
its progress has come to an end, and that it is

capable of no higher growth in grace. These winters are sometimes long and very hard to bear, and we are tempted under their influence to lose faith in the paternal Providence that is ever seeking to lead us onward in the regenerate life. Evil spirits throng the mind at these seasons, striving to drag it downward into the insanity of despair. To escape the power of these wintry spirits we must wrap our spiritual bodies in the garments of truth, and quicken them by the faithful performance of our daily duties ; and some day when we are not looking for it, some hour when we are not aware, the light of the Divine Sun will suddenly flash upon us, and its warmth thrill through us. Thus a new cycle of life will begin for us with its succession of seasons, whose history will form a new chapter in the Book of our life.

The length of these spiritual seasons varies with each individual ; but as the regenerate life advances, its winters become shorter and milder, and its periods of hope and fruition longer and more delightful.

If we heartily believe that this life is a preparation for the life to come, and death a door through which we pass from a world of types and things transient, into a world of realities and things permanent, and if we live lives in harmony with this belief, the advancing age of the body will not be painful to us. As we pass through the autumn of life, and feel its winter approaching, we shall not dwell upon the idea that our hands are losing their cunning and our feet their firmness of step; that our sight is becoming dim, and our ear forgetting to hear, and that we are sinking downward into the grave. Such thoughts belong to those who have built their houses upon the sand, and laid up their treasures upon earth. If they come to us we shall put them away as temptations from below, and we shall feel that our Heavenly Father is gently loosing the material bonds that connect us with this world, in order that we may turn our hearts towards the mansions He has prepared for us in the heavens. As our material eye becomes dim to the things of the earth, the spiritual eye within it will learn to see more clearly the things which pertain to heaven; and as our ear grows dull to earthly noises, it will listen more intently to the words of eternal life. All that we lose of the material will serve to quicken our sensibilities to the spiritual, and instead of wasting our thoughts in vain regrets for the earth which we are leaving, we shall be looking forward in joyful hope to the heaven we are about to enter.

It is a remark often made, that one would like to live so long as the faculties remain bright and the health firm; but these attributes being just those which prevent us from being willing to die, Providence kindly takes them from us, that, feeling the imperfections of the material body, we may become willing to put it off, and so come into the superior life of the spiritual body.

The poet Waller beautifully expresses this truth in a single couplet :—

> "The soul's dark cottage, batter'd and decay'd,
> Lets in new light through chinks that time has made.

The trouble is, that we are too prone to shiver and complain about the inclemencies that we feel through these chinks, instead of looking for the heavenly light that comes to us through them if we will but seek for it.

My garden, with its withered flowers and barrenness of fruit, is no longer a pleasant place to walk in for anything contained within its narrow limits, and I will not pretend that I can look without regret upon the havoc that the frost has made; but I can certainly bear it with much more patience, and even with some degree of contentment, as I look beyond it and see what the falling of the leaves from the elms that surround me has revealed. Through the bare but stately boughs I can trace the graceful outlines of the surrounding hills, rising one beyond another in the most charming variety, clad here and there with fine woods, or ornamented with trees, standing solitary or in groups, glowing with autumn colors, their brilliancy softened into the most exquisite tenderness of hue by the delicate haze that fills the air and saves the eye from being pained and dazzled by excess of brightness. Beyond this I can trace the horizon where heaven seems to clasp hands with earth, and to say, " Come up hither." Over all bends the dome of the sky, the view of its hemisphere now scarcely interrupted by the delicate tracery of the tree-tops, so that I can watch at will the motions of the clouds and of " the greater and the lesser lights."

I cannot but feel sorry that the season of flowers and fruits is departing ; but the joyous smiles with which it leaves us promise a speedy return ; and I should be unwilling to lose all this autumnal beauty, rich as it is in spiritual suggestions, even though I might have summer always.

AUTUMN LEAVES.

" Let the dead past bury its dead."—LONGFELLOW.

X.

AUTUMN LEAVES.

THE brightness of Autumn is gone, and the fallen leaves, brown and sear, scattered everywhere as they rustle beneath our footsteps, remind us, either sadly or thoughtfully, as the mind's tendency may be, of the beauty that has passed away. If we choose to take a sad view of life and nature, we can find apt illustration for our moody and morbid fantasies in the suggestions the withered leaves will furnish us; and as we crush them under our feet, the sound they give forth will be mournful to us as a funeral bell, telling us only of death and desolation.

All sorrowful views of the inevitable changes that Providence has ordained to take place in this world are, however, either mistaken or superficial; and if we find ourselves saddened by them, we should seek to understand them more wisely, and we shall then be very sure to find everywhere beauty instead of ashes.

Leaves correspond to truths, and withered leaves to the truths that, belonging to the external memory, pass out from our immediate cognizance, but are still ours when we wish to recall them for some special purpose.

Our thoughts are occupied every day by a succession of truths bearing upon our duties, employments, or amusements; and these truths, for the most part, seem to be of little or no value excepting for the moment; yet they are all important to the moment. Small as they are, it is the constant repetition of the impressions received from them that makes up the whole external of our minds, clothing them as the leaves clothe the trees. They pass away from us day by day, and even hour by hour; and to the superficial observer the truths that occupied the thoughts yesterday are of as little consequence to-day as last year's leaves are to the trees in the greenness of a present summer.

The cultivator finds that nothing nourishes the growth of plants so well as decayed leaves, and that each variety of plant is best nourished by its own decayed leaves. Herein we find a perfect correspondence between the plant and the human being. It is the accumulation of truths or facts filling the thoughts day by day that produces experience, and it is our own personal experience that builds up our mental strength and gives the most perfect growth in wisdom. The thoughtful person is like a careful cultivator, who gathers up the fallen leaves and uses them to nourish his plants ; but the thoughtless person is like one who suffers the idle winds to blow away the leaves, or perchance sets fire to them. The one is constantly gathering into the garner of his experience truths taught him by the successes and even by the failures of to-day, whereby to guide his life to-morrow ; while the other, reflecting upon nothing, adds nothing to his mental stores, and taking no thought about the mistakes of to-day, repeats them again to-morrow.

The past is a beneficent teacher to us if we look to it thoughtfully, seeking to find instruction for the present and future, and never allowing ourselves to dwell upon its disappointments and its sorrows with morbid regret, or upon its successes with proud rejoicing. If we would gain true wisdom from the past, we must study it, constantly bearing in mind that it was all overruled by

Providence ; that it was not our unaided strength that gained the battles of life, or won its prizes ; and that it was no idle chance that disappointed our hopes, or took from us our treasures.

Life is made up of a very few great events scattered among a multitude of small ones. From the small ones we may gather intelligence to guide us through the daily duties of our lives, and from the great ones we may attain wisdom that shall make our way plain in the darkest places through which we may be called to pass.

In order that the experience of the past may form a healthful nutriment for the life of the present, we must look back upon it without wishing for its return, and with eyes not blinded by regretful tears. It is only when the past has become dead to us that it can help to make us live. While we strive to keep the past alive by clinging to its memory with sighs and tears, wishing we could make it return to us, and losing our consciousness of the present, so far as we can, by dwelling in the world of memory, the past can only nourish our morbid passions, and unfit us for every duty. When, on the contrary, we give up the past as something not to be mourned for or wished back again, because our Heavenly Father has placed it **beyond our power,** making it irrevocable, and as it were dead, then it begins to give us life, and to nourish our **souls by its very decay.** Then we gather our dead leaves, **not to weep over** them, but to gain new **life from them.**

It is a **tendency of the merely natural mind to** cling with fondness **to the memory of the past, as** **if** the present could not give us anything **so desirable** as the pleasures **and blessings we have already** enjoyed. It believes the careless gayety **of childhood to be better than the developed usefulness** and tranquil **pleasures of mature life. It depreciates** the manners **and morals of the present day** in comparison with **those that prevailed formerly;** and rarely **finds in** a present blessing compensation **for** the loss of a former **one. It esteems mourning** for the dead **a sacred duty, and clothes** itself in sable weeds, **the livery of an insubordinate will,** that help **to keep up the delusion that** God does **not wisely number our days, and mercifully overrule the issues of life. Just so far as we give way** to these natural **tendencies of the mind,** we check its spiritual **growth, because we put ourselves in** direct **opposition to the eternal law of progress** which **the Creator has ordained for everything that He has made. A never-resting** movement is the tenure by which we hold our lives. If we pause anywhere our intelligence stagnates, our affections rust, our powers are dwarfed, and our faculties paralyzed. To desire to be always a child is to desire to be a mental dwarf. To hope to abide in any term of growth, or to enjoy always the self-same happiness, is to hope to place a bar beyond which our development shall not pass. To wish that our friends or ourselves might never die, is to wish that they and we may never know the highest culture, the purest happiness, the noblest useful-ness, of which humanity is capable. To talk of untimely death, of premature departure from this world, is to deny an overruling Providence, or to put our judgment above His.

The leaf falls from the tree because the bud of a future leaf swells beneath the end of its stem, and pushes it off from the bough. It has done its appointed work, and must make way for another that can perform the work that is yet to be done. The truths that clothe the mind as the leaves clothe the trees, forming the whole texture of the thoughts, change like the leaves if we make any mental growth. New relations in life, new objects of pursuit, new associates, new books, new vicis-situdes, everything in short that makes one day different from another, introduces new thoughts into the mind, and pushes out the old ones, and by these changes our minds grow, if they grow at all. Each time that the tree puts on a new covering of leaves, a new ring is added to the wood of its stem, and its branches spread higher toward heaven. What the trees do thus involuntarily, they do, under Providence, for our instruction; and if we accept the lesson they teach we shall pass through life's seasons striving to mourn as little as possible for the past, but so strengthened and quickened by its experience that our faith in the unslumbering love and unerring wisdom of our Heavenly Father will constantly become more firmly fixed, and our aspirations rise more ardently towards the heavenly mansions.

THE USES OF GARDENING.

The culture of plants, whether in-doors or out, affords a recreation to the mind so innocent in itself, and so suggestive of wise thought in its relations to all other culture, that the refraining from it seems a neglect of privilege, if not of duty.

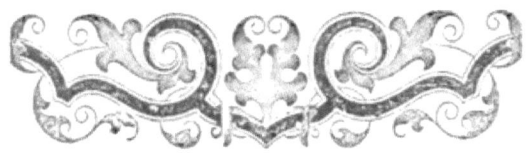

XI.

THE USES OF GARDENING.

NOW that the earth is so thickly covered with snow that I can no longer go out into my garden, I try to continue something of my connection with the vegetable world by having a few plants in the house. These are perhaps all the dearer to me that there are so few of them, and that they are so dependent on my care; since now nature gives them only light, while water and heat must come to them by artificial means. When plants become members of the household they are brought into a nearer relation to us, and seem more like personal friends than when they are in the garden. In the abundance of summer foliage and flowers we do not think so much of individual beauty as of the universal luxuriance of nature. We gather bouquets at will, to adorn our rooms, and so soon as they begin to fade we throw them

away with little remorse or regret; for there are
plenty more to supply their place.   In the winter,
with perhaps only a dozen plants, every leaf becomes a personal acquaintance, and a blossom is
an intimate friend, watched over with loving interest from the time the tiny bud is first discovered
till the faded petals droop and die.

However keenly we may enjoy the abounding
beauty that surrounds us in the prosperity of summer, there is an interior delight in the pleasures
we receive from nature in the adversity of winter,
that often touches the soul far more deeply.   Uninterrupted prosperity and unlimited affluence too
often produce but an imperfect growth of the
mind, because it enjoys them without reflection.
One pleasure succeeds another too rapidly to leave
space for thought between them.   The mind grows
under their influence like a fruit-tree planted in
fine soil, but which has never been pruned.   There
will probably be a luxuriant growth of wood and
foliage, but few blossoms and still fewer fruits.   If
nature gives us less to enjoy in winter than in
summer, she allows us more time to follow out
her suggestions; and if we do so faithfully, we
shall find that many of the thoughts we gain from
her, like many of the best sorts of pears and

apples, ripen only in the house. The household
is a garden where human development goes on in
a way corresponding to the growth of the animal
and the vegetable world; and it is through the
various relations the household involves, that we
best learn to apply to life the truths we gather in
our studies out of doors.

Most persons suppose that gardening, as a
pleasure, is a merely optional thing, and not a
question with which conscience has anything to
do; but there is a right and a wrong to most
questions, and to me it seems that not to have a
garden, where it is practicable, and not to have
plants in the house, which is almost always practicable, is neglecting to make use of a very important means of mental and moral culture.

We may receive the doctrines that Swedenborg
has unfolded in relation to the correspondences of
the vegetable kingdom in a general way, by simply
reading about them; but when we study them by
the actual observation of plants, we gain a knowledge of them incomparably more clear and vivid
than abstract study can give. If a chemist or
other student of natural science should confine
himself to books, refusing to make use of a labor-
atory, or to examine specimens of the animal,

vegetable, or mineral kingdoms about which he studied, affirming that he could learn just as well from books, every one conversant with such subjects would exclaim at his folly. Is it not a folly much more to be shunned, when one who believes in the science of correspondences, neglects the observation of natural objects offered so freely to him by the beneficent Creator? It is nearly twenty years since I became a reader of Swedenborg, and it is only two years that I have had a garden; but I think I do not exaggerate when I say that in these two years, through the aid my garden has given me, I have learned more about correspondences than in the whole preceding eighteen.

Not long before I had a garden of my own, I remarked to an enthusiastic horticulturist, who was talking to me of his fruits and flowers, "You must find great pleasure in your garden." "Not pleasure only," said he, "but culture also." I did not comprehend at that time what he meant, and was surprised at his reply. I had not, however, enjoyed my own garden a month before my eyes began to open, for I found that my garden was educating me in the true sense of the word; leading out my faculties by suggesting new trains of thought, and illustrating old and new thoughts

by correspondences so exquisite, that I felt introduced through them into a new world.

One may love flowers, and enjoy them as they
grow under the care of other hands; but plants
are like children; they tell their secrets only to
those who show their love by doing something for
them; and the more one does, so it be done for
love, the more secrets one hears and sees.

Many suppose that things may be appreciated
by contemplation, apart from action; but when
they experiment actively in these same things,
their senses are opened, and they discover that
hitherto they have had eyes but saw not, ears but
heard not. Abstract knowledge is automatic and
external, while practical knowledge is living and
internal. What we learn practically becomes a
part of ourselves, and results in something that
remains with us forever.

Thus has it been with my garden. I began it
merely as an amusement, but found it a true
recreation. I began thinking only of cultivating
it; and, to my surprise, found it immediately
began to cultivate *me.* I hoped to find bodily
health from working in it, and found mental health
far more.

There has always been a belief in the popular

mind that the odor of freshly cultivated earth possessed a health-giving power, and feeble children
are thought to be invigorated by " playing in the
dirt." I am convinced that this popular opinion
is no fallacy, for my own experience has proved to
me that the breath of our mother earth is a tonic
of surprising power.

It was a fable of the Greek Mythology, that
when Antæus, the son of Earth and Ocean, con-
tended with an enemy, as often as he was thrown
upon the ground, his mother gave him strength to
renew the combat until he was victorious. Since
I have become intimate with mother Earth, and
have experienced her renovating power, I have
felt as though the Greeks symbolized the hygienic
force of the soil in the fable, and that Antæus was
but a type of all of us who wrestle in the garden
and in the field to escape from the thrall of in-
validism. I have found health, recreation, and
mental culture in my garden; and I write my
experiences in the hope that it may draw others to
seek the same blessings from the same source. I
will not promise them to any one save upon condition that they are sought lovingly, as a child
goes to its mother for aid. I believe the earth is
a beneficent mother to those who go to her with a

truly filial feeling ; but if you have no love for her,
—if no answering emotion rises in your breast
when she clothes herself in her beautiful garments,
and offers you her bounty of flowers and fruits, I
will promise you nothing for all the toil you may
expend. If you have lost your health, you must
go to the druggist for help, for your heart is too
cold and your brain too heavy to be permeated by
the soft, life-giving breath that renews the being
of every true child of Earth, when he turns lovingly towards his mother.

Everything that is high in the creation contains
within itself everything that is lower ; we are all
that is below us and something more, and the
something more is what gives us our distinctive
individuality.

We are born children of the Earth, and we do
not cease to be such when we become spiritualized.
The external of our spirit draws its nutriment
from the external world, and we do not leave it
behind us as we live more in the internal ; but we
fill it with a higher life. Thus our enjoyment of
everything beautiful becomes indefinitely heightened
in proportion as our affections and thoughts become purified and elevated ; and the more brightly
light comes down to us from heaven, the more

distinctly are we able to read the book of nature, and to perceive that it was written by the hand of God. Irreverent minds are confirmed in their indifference to spiritual things by the study of nature. They look down till they lose the power of looking up; and sometimes dwell upon the wonders of creation till they deny a Creator; but the reverent eye scans the heavens all the more steadfastly if the feet are planted firmly upon the earth; and finds a new incentive to worship in every fact of science and every form of nature.

Formerly I cared little for house-plants; but now I feel as though they were indispensable, and that I must have a little garden in the house, when the severity of the season compels me to desert the garden out of doors. All the phases of plant-growth correspond perfectly with those of the mind; and the more carefully we watch them, the better are we able to understand the development of the mental powers, and to gain true ideas in relation to the training of our own faculties, and the directing of other minds over whom our influence may extend.

A mother would find an hour a day spent among her flowers, a very useful preparation for the hours she spends with her children. It is a great mistake, too often made by mothers, that hours spent apart from the cares in which their families involve them are stolen hours, to which they have scarce a right. Apart from the instruction to be derived from the tending of plants, the relaxation of the mind from care past, and its re-creation for care to come, renew the life of the mind, and through that the life of the body; so that more would be accomplished in the hours that are left, than if that one had not been taken from them. Do not, then, if you are a mother with many cares, deny yourself the pleasure and benefit of plants, because you think you have not time for them.

You may as well forbid your children to take advantage of the recess at school, hoping that they will learn more from studying all the time they are at school, as to deny yourself the recess from care in your long days at home, supposing that you can accomplish more by uninterrupted effort. The child can learn more when he has a proper recess during his school hours, and the mother can do more, with less effort and less fatigue, if she too has a recess from her cares. A little time spent with your plants each day, will unbend your mind from the strain perpetual care brings upon it, and will rest your eyes, which are so apt to be overtasked; and by giving a new turn to your thoughts, for a little while, will reanimate you to return to your family duties. You will come back to your work with new alacrity, as the child comes into the house, from his play, all alive and joyous.

The early passing away of youth in the women of America has long been observed, and various causes have been assigned for it. I am convinced that it is the want of relaxation from family cares. Whenever I have observed a woman who retains her youthful appearance, I have always found she had some special taste that drew her away from her cares. It might be music, or painting, or reading; but always something apart from the daily requirements of her life. She, perhaps, indulged her taste by stealth, and doubting if she were right in doing so; but the wrong is to refrain from such indulgence. Mind and body suffer alike for lack of it, and the dwelling place becomes, through unremitted toil, a weary house of bondage, instead of a free and happy home.

THE HOUSEHOLD GARDEN.

"Home is the source, channel, issue, of all those principles and powers which bless earth and promise immortality. The inmost of the circles which spread out widening, and, amidst change, still enduring, into societies, nations, churches, and whatever forms humanity may receive."—T. T. STONE.

XII.

THE HOUSEHOLD GARDEN.

THE correspondence existing between the mind of man and the forms and operations of the natural world, is frequently referred to in the Scriptures. The righteous man is compared to "a tree planted by the rivers of water." The obedient are encouraged with the promise that "their soul shall be as a watered garden." The sowing of seed, the springing up of the blade, the production of fruit, are made to illustrate the planting of truth in the mind and the results that come from it, according to the quality of the mind in which it is planted. The garden may be considered as representing a society of human beings, in which each plant represents an individual; or it may be looked upon as one man, the earth of it corresponding to the mind, and the various plants representing its different traits. In either case the

(147)

correspondence is perfect, as the Scriptures testify. The institution of a society for any purpose is thus the planting of a garden, and in order that it may succeed it must be well chosen as to soil, and then it must be watered by heavenly truth, and warmed by heavenly love. If a society is ineffectual for the purposes for which it was organized, it is because it is deficient in one or more of these requisites. It looks perhaps to self for light, instead of turning to the Lord : and is warmed by hatred for evil, rather than by love for goodness.

Of all the social gardens with which the earth is planted, none is so important in its results to the whole fabric of society, none so powerful in its influence upon individual life, as the household. The political, the moral, and the religious life of a nation depend upon the influences that gather round the homesteads of its people. The seeds there sown will spring up into plants and trees that will be transplanted into larger spheres, to grow into forms of beauty and of use, bearing flowers and fruits that shall minister to the wants and to the pleasures of all who surround them ; or else into perverted and hateful deformities, ready to poison the atmosphere and blast the touch, wherever their influence may be borne.

The household is the only social garden in which every human being has a personal interest; and this fact alone is sufficient to prove that it is the most important of them all.

The salvation of the souls of men is the first object in the Providence of God; and as the setting of human beings in families is a universal arrangement of His Providence, it seems a natural inference that the influences coming to the soul through the family relations are those which most powerfully effect its growth and development.

We cannot look around us without being forced to acknowledge that a large proportion of families are organized in such a way, that no true development of the soul is effected through their means. This want of success is not always the result of depravity. Many earnestly desire and strive to bring up their children wisely, and to fulfil all the family relations as they should; and yet they fail. Many more take no proper thought about their duties; but go on at random, satisfied if they do about as well as their neighbors, and thinking it no fault of theirs when their children disappoint their hopes. The variety of mistaken culture every social circle affords is so painful, that sometimes those who are childless are tempted to congratulate themselves; since they thereby escape a responsibility which so few are able to bear with success.

It is commonly believed that moral science is not exact and positive, like the sciences that deal with material objects; and that cause and effect do not cling together in human development as in the growth of plants and animals. If I assert the contrary belief, it may be brought against me that not having had personal experience in training a family, my opinion is of little value. Still the subject is one that has deeply interested me all my life, and the very fact of having no family of my own has left me time and opportunity to extend my observations over a wider circle of the families of other people; so that I build my theories upon a foundation of facts far more numerous than if I had been experimenting at home.

My leading theory is briefly this. The parents of every family control the characters of their children with a power corresponding to that which a cultivator of the soil exercises over his farm or his garden; and the limitations of this power are in like manner corresponding.

Humanity is nowhere omnipotent. "Paul may plant, and Apollos may water; but it is God who giveth the increase." God works constantly in two ways, directly and indirectly: through human means and overruling human means. The gardener is not certain of success in all his efforts, let him work diligently and wisely as he can. Some of his plants will die, and some of them will repay his toil but meagrely; still, taking all things together, his reward is, on the whole, proportionate with his efforts.

A gardener who wishes to excel in his profession must make a study of the science of gardening, and then he must learn the art of applying that science. The scientific and the practical must ever go hand in hand, in order to attain to excellence. So the parent who would really educate a child must have a definite knowledge of what he is aiming at; and then he must pursue his object by means adapted to the end to be attained.

When two persons unite their destinies for life with the same kind of thoughtlessness that they would take partners for a cotillon, and then bring up children as heedlessly as if they were not responsible beings, they have as much right to complain of their want of success, as a gardener who buys a lot of land without seeing it, and cultivates it only in the night.

Plants sown at random, and children brought up without care, sometimes turn out well, because other influences reach them, and do for them what their natural protectors failed of doing; but the possibility of such a result does not in the least diminish the responsibility of those to whom the duty of training rightly belongs. The sin of their neglect hangs as heavily about their necks as if it resulted in the failure it deserved.

Humanity loves to sit at ease, and to find excuses for putting off, or setting aside, its duties. Those who yield to their indolent tendencies have no right to complain that life with them is a failure, and that their children bring their gray hairs in sorrow to the grave: but to those who look life, with all its responsibilities, calmly in the face; who feel the Divine Providence always and everywhere surrounding them; who seek to know the law of the Lord that they may do and teach it, ascribing the power and glory always to the Lord, failure is almost impossible.

The majority of parents begin their duties with no fixed principles, with little knowledge of their own hearts, and still less of that most delicate of all organizations, the heart of a little child. Not accustomed to the control of their own evil dis-

positions, they begin by indulging the evil disposi-
tions of their child, until they clash with their
own; and then, mistaking violence for power,
they resort to angry words or blows to exorcise
the evil spirits their own neglect has permitted to
take possession of their child. They rely on the
evil spirits that infest themselves to cast out those
that infest their children. Then the household becomes a field of battle, in which anger and violence
are the overruling powers, in which there is nothing of confidence on either side; in which the
child grows up cunning, deceitful, and false; and
the parents, simply because they reap the natural
harvest of the seed they sowed, deny that children
are a blessing, as they sink morosely into the old
age that feels itself in the way of all that is young,
because it has no sympathy with the perennial
pleasures of innocence.

Another class of parents, of a naturally gentle
disposition, by their devotion to their children
pamper their selfishness until they develop characters the direct opposite of their own. Society
looks on and says: "Here is a mother who has
given up all social pleasures to take the whole care
of her children upon herself, and her sons are
growing up dissipated and worthless, and her

daughters thinking of nothing but dress and display. What has she gained by all this self-sacrifice?" The truth seems to me to be that she has gained just what she had a right to expect. Her love for her children was a mere natural impulse. She devoted herself to them because she loved them with her whole heart and soul and mind and strength; as if they were her very own, and not recollecting that they were confided to her care by one who bids us love Him first, and make His Word the law of our lives. Parental affection is but a blind guide when it walks by its own insight; and is very sure to lead the way into tangled woods, and bewildering mazes that end in destruction.

Parental love, when viewed superficially, seems more free than any other from the taint of selfishness. During infancy and early childhood, parents often seem to live only for ministering to the wants and pleasures of their offspring; but even here selfishness may be the life of all this devotion. The child is but a part, an expansion of self; and just as parents love themselves so they love their children. Wilful, self-indulgent parents love to pamper the wilfulness and self-indulgence of their children; vain parents inflate the vanity of their

children; worldly parents train their children to
worldliness; and so on through the whole cata-
logue of vices. There is no more virtue in such
love than in that of the pickpocket who teaches his
child to steal; or the drunkard who pets his child
with a taste of his drams. The only difference is,
that one parent teaches vulgar vices, while the
other teaches the vices of refined society.

When the child becomes of an age to manifest
its own thoughts and desires independently of the
parent, the difficulty that the parent often feels in
yielding the child its just freedom, in acknowledging the liberty that belongs to it as a child of God,
—a liberty that should not be denied it, when it
becomes of an age to judge for itself, because then
it becomes accountable to an authority higher than
that of the earthly parent,—proves the selfishness
that may lie hidden within even a mother's devotion.

The loves of dominion and of possession too
often give a zest to parental love. We love that
which is ductile in our hands, that which yields itself to our power; and we love that which belongs
to ourselves because it is in reality a part of self.

When the loves of self and of the world rule in
the heart of the parents, the natural products of

the houschold garden are offensive flowers and bitter fruits ; but where love to the Lord rules supremely, and His Word is the household law,
home becomes an Eden, a genuine garden of God,
wherein no leaf shall wither and no fruit shall
blast.

HOME VIRTUES.

"To the child, the parent stands as the embodied reason, the form of truth and virtue, the highest type of the Supreme Being."

T. T. Stone.

XIII.

HOME VIRTUES.

THE natural affections, such as conjugal, parental, filial, and fraternal love, and the love of home, which would seem to bind all the others into a single sheaf of household virtues, are supposed by many persons to be inherently and of necessity pure and holy. Yet every one of these affections may be only modifications of the love of self. Self-love clings, like the Pilgrim's burden, to every trait of our nature ; and can be cast off only at the foot of the cross. Natural affection, until it has been spiritualized by regeneration, is a body without a soul, the form of love without its immortal essence.

We may test the quality of any of our affections, by honestly answering such questions as the following : Does it make us love to minister to others, or demand that others should minister to us? Do we seek our own happiness in loving, or the happiness of the person we love? Do we love to be at home, because there we can rule, and fret, and find fault without restraint, and devote ourselves to our own pleasure; or because there we reciprocate all kindly affections, and help to fill out the harmony of a happy household?

We are all prone to love those who flatter our vanity, who pet our foibles and weaknesses, who look with an indulgent eye upon our vices, or who minister to our comfort; and among our family relatives, we usually find more of all this than in any other social circle. We love to be ministered to, and to exercise selfishness in many ways, and a very ardent love of home may dwell in our hearts, because there we are ministered to more than elsewhere — because there we can be more selfish than anywhere else.

If the love of dominion and of selfish indulgence were put away from the human heart, a home would be more delightful from containing a numerous family, and involving every variety of relationship; because the various faculties of the heart would be called into more complete activity, and a fuller and higher life attained, than is possible in a small home circle. The affections

lose their pliancy and expansiveness by being confined within narrow limits; and it is more difficult
to avoid becoming more indulgent towards ourselves, and less so towards others, in a small
household, where there are few interests, than in
a large one, where there are many.

A happy home, like heaven, is a place where
each individual is seeking to make others happy.
There is no class of persons who find so little happiness as those who seek it directly, through self-
indulgence of any kind; no matter how innocent
the mode of indulgence may be. Self-forgetful-
ness is the first, and a desire to benefit others the
second, requisite in a happy life. We must think
of ourselves in order to cultivate our powers
of usefulness, our moral and intellectual faculties,
and to keep our bodies in a state of health, that
they may may be able to serve the mind; and we
shall find happiness in such thoughts of ourselves;
but the moment we begin to form plans of life that
have our own individual happiness as means and
end, we are taking the most direct method of making ourselves miserable. Just so far as the members of a household seek their happiness in making
others happy, home becomes a correspondence
of heaven; and just so far as they seek their own

11

individual happiness without regard, or in opposition to, the happiness of the rest, home becomes a correspondence of hell.

Parents who would make home a heavenly abode, must bear in mind that they are to the little child what the Heavenly Father is to themselves. A little child's only idea of God is based upon the ideas of love, wisdom, and power that he receives from the daily life of his father and mother. A child who sees his parents religiously self-controlled, and just and affectionate, will be sure to respect and love and obey them, and the filial virtue they arouse in his mind will form a generous soil, on which piety and reverent obedience to God will spring up and grow until they overshadow the whole being. But if the child is so unfortunate as to see his parents without self-control; if they indulge or thwart his wishes in accordance with the mood of their own tempers, and without regard to propriety and justice; if they deny him at first, and then yield to his teasing importunities; if they tell him to do right, and yet permit him to do wrong; if they pet him when they feel good-natured, and scold him when they feel cross, it is impossible that he should have any feeling of true respect for them. He may love

them fitfully, as they love him; and he will obey
them when he cannot help it; and all this prepares
him to think of God as an arbitrary being, very
fearful and terrible, and altogether removed from
the plane of his love.

A little child is almost intuitively pious, if the
least help is given him by those who are about
him; for the angels that continually behold the
face of the Heavenly Father, are lending all their
influence to draw his heart upward; and if his
earthly guardians would but coöperate with his
heavenly ones, his spiritual growth would be as
certain and as easy as his material growth. His
course would not be steadily upward, because the
soul has its natural and inherited diseases like
the body; and these will, from time to time, be
brought out by temptation, as the physical diseases incident to childhood are developed by favor-
ing circumstances; but these would all be miti-
gated by a previously wise training, and overcome
by wise treatment, with much more success in the
mental education than in the physical; because
the will has far more power to modify the traits of
the mind than of the body. In order to develop
true filial respect in the minds of children, parents
must first have developed a true and childlike

piety in themselves. They must recognize their own responsibility to their Heavenly Father before they can see clearly to direct the hearts of the little beings whom He has intrusted to their care. The child has no reason or conscience of its own ; and they must be reason and conscience for him.

Parental authority, during the first few years of the child's life, should be entirely arbitrary. Reason and conscience develop slowly in a child, through instruction and training. Until they are developed he should be made implicitly obedient to the reason and conscience of his parents. To tell a child that an act is foolish or wrong, and then to let him do it, is throwing a responsibility from the parent, who ought to bear it, upon the child, who is too weak to bear it. Every time this is done the child is confirmed in indifference to wrong, and in contempt of parental authority. If the parent has too little self-control to enforce obedience in a child, it is much better to let him alone entirely than to attempt to throw off the responsibility which belongs entirely to the parent. The selfish weakness that attempts to quiet its own conscience, by merely telling a child it is wrong to do anything, and then permitting him to do it, is just as reprehensible as acknowledging a thing to be wrong and then doing it one's self. There are persons who seem to think it mitigates the sin of an evil act, if one confesses it to be wrong; but to sin in the face of conviction is something that admits of no palliation. If you have so little moral strength that you will not enforce obedience in your child, at least have the forbearance to let him sin ignorantly. Do not confirm him in disobedience towards yourself, and in indifference to right and wrong, by laying burdens of responsibility upon his shoulders that he is wholly unable to bear. Your child cannot appreciate the consequences of a wrong action, because he has had almost no experience or observation of life; you know what the consequences are, and it is your duty to shield him from them by preventing him from doing wrong. We, who are grown men and women, all know how hard it is to resist the evil desires of our own hearts, although we can measure the consequences of indulging them so fully; and yet we wonder that a little child is not ready to put away his evil desires the moment we tell him they are wrong. His passions about little things are just as hard for him to resist as our greater passions about greater things; while his ignorance of consequences is almost total. He needs every aid we can give him to prevent his little feet from stumbling over the pebbles in his pathway, that to our greater strength are scarcely noticeable. We must not think we have done our duty, because we have told him of the danger. It is for us to hold him up, till he can walk safely by his own strength; to restrain him, till by degrees he learns to restrain himself; to guide him till he has learned all we can teach him of the right way.

Simple obedience is the only virtue a little child can practise, and it is the foundation of every other virtue. The child should be trained to it in the very first year of its existence; with all possible tenderness, but with equal firmness. Every month that this training is put off its difficulty increases; and lost time and opportunity are two things that can never be recovered. Be very careful that you are right in what you require of your child, and then bear in mind that just in the degree it is right, you will be wrong if you do not enforce obedience in him.

It is not always easy to know exactly what is right, and how much one should require of a little child. The more one lives a life of childlike obedience to the Heavenly Father, the better one understands what to ask of one's child; and to do this, one must keep as near Him as possible, through prayer and study of His Word. He is nearer to the parent than the parent is to the child; and if the heart is opened to Him, he will teach it "wondrous things out of His law."

PARENTAL DUTY.

"Remember how sacred childhood is; no ground so holy, no temple so reverent: God is within. Far off from the hallowed scene, let profaneness, irreverence, unkindness, pass and disappear."—T. T. STONE.

XIV.

PARENTAL DUTY.

I HAVE said that parental government should at first be entirely arbitrary. How long it should continue so must depend upon the rapidity with which the mental powers of the child unfold themselves. If you attempt to reason with a child, in order to convince his understanding of the difference between right and wrong, before he is old enough to appreciate what you say, you will confuse and worry him if he is of a mild disposition, and you will confuse and irritate him if he is combative. In neither case have you made obedience easier to him or control easier to yourself. You must judge of the use of your reasoning by the effect it produces, and not be impatient to see your child a man in comprehension, while he is scarcely more than an infant in years. Very early development of conscience or reason in a child is .

(171)

almost always the result of a diseased brain ; and should never be sought for nor encouraged. The memoirs of pious little children, so often found in juvenile libraries, would be far more appropriate in the library of the medical student ; for they illustrate a peculiar form of disease, and not a healthy growth.

If your child at seven years of age is affectionate and obedient, you should be content with him, though he does not accurately reason about right and wrong. Affection and obedience will go hand in hand with the child, if the power you have exercised over him has been truly parental. If you find him fearful towards you, seeking to avoid you in his pursuits, and silent and constrained in your presence, you have made a mistake somewhere. You have exercised too much power or too little affection, or you have not sympathized enough in his pursuits and pleasures ; or perhaps you have laughed at him, which, to a sensitive child, is of all hard things the hardest to bear. You may be content with your child if he is simply obedient, but do not be content with yourself unless he is affectionate also. If he loves you as a companion in his walks and his talks and his sports, and yet is obedient to you when you do not indulge him in his wishes, then it is well with the child and with you also.

Different children require very different modes of training. In the vegetable world, not only do different species of plants require different modes of treatment, but even different varieties of the same species. What will be entirely favorable to one kind of apple or pear, will be entirely destructive to another. So with children in the same family; one needs to be encouraged, and another to be restrained; one needs protection, while another is as well or better without it; some are discouraged by opposition, while to others it is exciting; and so on with endless variety. To do justice to a family of children, much thought must be given to their peculiarities. The father and mother must not feel that when they have provided for the material wants of the children, and sent them to school, they have done what is most important. Careful and troubled about the many things that constitute the comfort of life they may have been, but there is one thing absolutely needful; and if they would choose the better part they must not exhaust all their strength and thought in providing for that which belongs only to this world.

Children are not gifts to be held as your personal property, and to do with as you please. You hold them simply in trust from the Lord; and you will have presently to account to Him for the care you have taken of them. He is saying to you in His Holy Word now, just as authoritatively as He said to the disciples when He walked openly in Judea: "Suffer little children to come unto me." Are you leading them to Him, or are you shutting them out from Him? You are doing one of these things, for no parental influence is negative.

If the father of a family looks upon making money as the paramount duty of his life, and the mother puts keeping the house and clothing the children above all other duties, the lives of both are perpetually forbidding the little children to come near the Lord. Most persons are obliged to spend their days in work for the support and comfort of the body, and industry is one of the greatest virtues; but this does not make it needful that the mind should be absorbed in work to the exclusion of everything else. Such a life is slavery of the basest kind, because self-assumed; and the more wealth that is accumulated by such labor, the more degrading becomes the bondage.

Some of the finest examples of parental education I have ever seen have been among persons who were compelled by poverty to lives of constant labor ; and no class of human beings afford examples more numerous or more reprehensible of parental neglect, than those whose wealth places them beyond the necessity of effort.

Perhaps I can best illustrate the ideas I wish to present by examples. There was once a family in the circle of my acquaintance, containing many children, the father and mother of whom, beginning in narrow circumstances, had arrived at a somewhat advanced age, their children grown up around them, and property enough laid by for an easy independence. Both parents had been indefatigably industrious, the one in his calling, the other in her household ; but their industry had limited itself, almost entirely, to life in its relations with this world. The mother had begun life with religious impressions and feelings, but the cares of this world overcame them, and choked them up. The children grew up indifferent to spiritual things, and with passions uncontrolled by principle. I was more than once present in this family when the most painful exhibitions were made of ill-temper and irreverence ; but on one such occasion the

mother turned to me, with tears in her eyes, and
said, " I have lived a life of toil and care for my
family, and I felt at the time that I was doing as
I ought; but now, in my old age, my children
prove to me that I have been unfaithful to my
highest duty." What a conviction to carry to
one's grave! Never, in the whole course of my
life, have I seen physical poverty or suffering that
seemed to me so pitiful as the spiritual destitution
and grief of that mother.

Another example will ever remain green in my
memory, of the mother of a large family of
young children, left a widow, and entirely destitute. She was a woman of profound religious
principle, and she took up her cross and bore it
steadfastly. Her children saw that she governed
herself and them from the highest and purest motives, and they followed as she led the way. A
life of patient industry still left her time to incul-
cate wise principles in the hearts of her children,
and they remained faithful to them. No black
sheep marred the beauty of her fold. She fed
the lambs intrusted to her care, remembering that
they belonged to the Lord; and the best success
has attended them thus far through life.

Such examples are not rare or peculiar. They

are types of the two great classes into which humanity is divided. The one sees this world only, and lives only for the favors and rewards that this world can give. The other is ever looking through and beyond the things of this world, and valuing them as leading to something higher, something eternal. I do not mean to say that one class is entirely worldly-minded, and the other entirely heavenly-minded; for absolute perfection or depravity does not belong to this world. What I mean is, that in every human being there is a central and supreme love that dominates over all the other affections, giving them an upward or a downward tendency, according as it aspires to heaven or clings to this world. In the social relations of life the character of this central love is not usually distinctly shown; but in the freedom of home it appears much more clearly, and it acts upon the impressible minds of children with very great power. Every time a child perceives that its parents do things to please society, or refrain from doing things through fear of society, he takes a lesson from them in worldly servility; and every time he perceives that they do things because they are right, or abstain from doing things because they are wrong, he takes a lesson in Christian freedom.

It is no uncommon thing for a child to be more severely scolded or punished for offending against manners than against morals. The parent is mortified and angry at the rudeness or awkwardness of a child, but only moderately sorry if he lies. The child soon learns to look upon rudeness as a greater offence than lying, and acts accordingly. In very little children lying is sometimes even laughed at as being very funny, or as showing great brightness. As the child grows older, and becomes confirmed in the habit, the parents begin to wonder at his depravity, and finally set it down as a general rule that all children are liars. Lying is no doubt a fearfully common vice; but so far as my observation has gone, it is much more common with grown people than with children. The difference between the true and the false is one of the earliest distinctions a child can appreciate, and the parent cannot be too careful in teaching him to speak the truth, both by example and precept. If a child finds that his parents are faithful in keeping their promises to him, and that they never deceive him in any way, he will respect the truth in them; and if he sees that falsehood always grieves and troubles them, he will be sure to avoid it. He should be taught that it is a sin against God to tell a lie, and therefore an act to be very sorry for. If parents are angry or violent towards a child, they destroy their moral power over him, and he looks upon what he has done as merely an offence against them. If they are impressed with a true feeling of reverence for God's law, they will not be angry when their child offends against it, but sorry; and their sorrow will awaken a true feeling of penitence in the child, which will make him strive to abstain from a repetition of his offence, with far more earnestness than could have been induced by any degree of anger or severity. Violence in the parent wakens only fear towards the parent, while it is fear of the sin that can alone regenerate the child's heart. Fear towards the parent will lead him to hide his wrong doings; but fear towards sin will lead him to put it away. He cannot be too early taught to feel the nearness of his Heavenly Father, and the impossibility of hiding anything from Him. Parents must, however, beware that their own lives show that they feel all that they teach; for if children find a nicer morality is expected from them than their parents practise in their own persons, they will soon see through and despise the hypocrisy. If you would make your child reverent, and obedient, and truthful, you must make your own life the exemplification of your teachings. You have no right to expect your child to be better than yourself; but if he should be,—for a child much oftener rises above his education than sinks below it,—you must remember that his respect for you must diminish in proportion as his virtue increases.

SIMPLE PLEASURES.

"We must sow the seeds, and tend the growth, if we would enjoy the flower."

"If happiness is the rarest of blessings, it is because the reception of it is the rarest of virtues."—SOUVESTRE.

XV.

SIMPLE PLEASURES.

AMONG the very small number of plants that has formed my winter garden are two rose-bushes, a Safrano and a Giant of Battles; the one the saffron yellow that we see occasionally in the sky at sunset, and the other so richly red that it reminds me of Herbert's stanza :

> "Sweet rose! whose hue, angry and brave,
> Bids the rash gazer wipe his eye :
> Thy root is ever in its grave ;—
>   And thou must die."

The plants are small, and have given me only one or two blossoms at a time ; but I have found so much pleasure in watching them, from the time the bud first formed until the petals unfolded their perfected beauty, that I have been drawn to think a good deal of the many pleasures with which this world abounds, and which we neglect to enjoy.

(183)

We look at a fine hot-house full of flowers and
think how delightful it must be to own such a
place ; and possibly, instead of enjoying its beauty
heartily, as we would that of a fine prospect, or a
glorious sky, that thought of possession embitters
our heart, and we turn moodily away, wondering
why God is so much more indulgent to our neighbor than He is to us.

Now it is my conviction that the enjoyment of
possessions does not increase in proportion to their
number and magnitude.   It does not seem to me
that persons who keep gardeners to take care of
their plants gain as much actual enjoyment from
them as I gain from mine, of which I take the entire care myself.   It is not the having things in
our possession merely that enables us to enjoy
them, but it is the way our affections are developed
by their means.   There is, to be sure, the base-
born pleasure of shining in the eyes of our neighbors, which may be gotten through fine houses, fine
clothes, fine gardens, or any possession we may
have ; but such pleasure is not happiness, and does
not involve the true enjoyment of anything that
we possess.   If we are vain of anything we have,
it is no longer that thing which gives us pleasure,

but only the admiration excited by it in our neighbors.

The true enjoyment of anything which helps to make us happy, is based upon the adaptation of that thing to the wants of our own minds, and is entirely independent of anything our neighbor may think about it.

The use of pleasure is to rest and recreate the mind, and our enjoyment of it is in exact proportion to the rest and recreation we get from it. One person may be surrounded by the greatest variety of luxuries, in houses, gardens, and grounds, of his own possession, and yet not get so much enjoyment and recreation from them as another will from strolling among simple scenes of nature, and contemplating earth and sky as God's glorious handiwork. When we give ourselves heartily up to the enjoyment of anything which, like the ocean, the sky, or a vast landscape, by its very nature precludes all thought of possession, we are lifted into a far higher enjoyment than when we can say, " How much I wish this was mine !" and if we cast all feelings of envy out from our hearts, we can enjoy the possessions of our neighbors as much as if they were our own. Vanity of our own possessions, and envy at those of our neighbor, are different expressions of the same vice. A man who is rich and vain, would be envious if he were poor; and the poor man who is envious will be sure to become vain if he become rich. With both it is the opinion of the neighbor that constitutes the value of all that is possessed.

Domestic happiness depends in a very great degree on the enjoyment that is derived from simple pleasures. If a mother devote herself entirely to work, she cannot make an attractive home for her husband and children, any farther than the wants of the body are concerned. A boy will like to come home at meal times, and to sleep, if his mother supplies him with good bed and board; but if that is all she prepares for him, he will seek entertainment in the streets at other hours, and each year of his life will find him less able to enjoy the innocent pleasures that belong to a happy home. A girl who sees her mother so devoted to household care that she allows herself no time for anything else, learns to look upon domestic duty as mere drudgery, and avoids it as far as she possibly can.

There is nothing children wish for so much as sympathy, and this can be given without interfering with any domestic avocation. There is nothing in sewing, or cooking, or washing, or ironing, that need absorb the thoughts so that a mother cannot talk to a child, or listen to its story-books, while she is engaged in them. I have observed that women who thus keep their sympathies open to their children do not grow nervous, and prematurely old, like those who fix their minds entirely upon the work that engages their hands, and who have only impatient words to give their children when they try to talk with them while they are at work.

There is nothing in the recollections of my own childhood that I look back upon with so much pleasure as the reading aloud my books to my mother. She was then a woman of many cares, and in the habit of engaging in every variety of household work. Whatever she might be doing in kitchen, or dairy, or parlor, she was always ready to listen to me, and to explain whatever I did not understand. There was always with her an under-current of thought about other things, mingling with all her domestic duties, lightening and modifying them, but never leading her to neglect them, or to perform them imperfectly. I believe it is to this trait of her character that she owes the elasticity and ready social sympathy that still animates her under the weight of almost four-score years. How much I owe to the care and sympathy she gave to my childish years, I cannot measure.

I am induced to speak of my own personal experience on this point because mothers not unfrequently deny that they can talk and work at the same time; and find in their various needful occupations a ready excuse for giving their children short answers, and keeping them away from their presence as much as possible. My purpose is to recommend nothing as a duty that I have not seen practised with success, and which I am not sure is entirely within the power of every parent who is willing to perform the duties belonging to that holy office.

But I have wandered very far away from the roses whence I set out, and which I intended to have made the leading text of my discourse.

The love of flowers is almost universal among children. The baby in its cradle stretches its tiny fingers eagerly after them, and the older child passes many of its happiest hours in seeking for wild-flowers. We always enjoy those possessions most which we have done something ourselves in order to obtain; and children at a very early age find not only an interesting, but a very valuable amusement in cultivating plants.

Our Heavenly Father gives the most valuable and the most beautiful of his gifts to us with an abounding liberality : light and air and water for the body, the glories of earth and sky for the soul ; the sky sown with stars, shining for every one of his children ; earth sown with flowers, blooming freely for all.

One of the purest of all the simple pleasures that go to make up domestic happiness, is the culture of flowers. They come within the means of every one. If you have a garden you can soon fill it with beautiful plants brought from the woods and fields, with no expense but the pleasure of collecting them. If you live in a city, and in the winter, whether in city or country, a few cents will give you a plant that will be a source of enjoyment to you for months ; and a few shillings will fill your window with them. Raising plants yourself, either from seeds or slips, is very easy ; and the process will be full of interest for your children. This interest may be greatly increased if you will get some simple work on Botany and read it with your children. Gray's " How Plants Grow," is the best book for this purpose that has ever been published, and simple as a child's talk. If the subject be new to you you will very probably find yourself desiring to know more about plants after you have made yourself acquainted with this charming little book; and if so, you will find the larger works by the same author full of interest. If you wish to understand how to manage your plants skilfully, Mrs. Loudon's "Ladies' Companion to the Flower-Garden" will probably answer every question you will wish to ask.

You will soon find that plants are not mere playthings; mere sources of amusement; but a cheering presence in your solitude, a manifold resource for pleasure and instruction with your children; and in watching the various stages of their growth, and the varying care they require, you will gain valuable suggestions for the mental as well as. physical training of yourself no less than of your children.   The development of thought and affection in the mind is so curiously analogous to vegetable growth, that plants are an endless source of instruction; and the more we learn from them, the more our perceptions are quickened for new discoveries.   A window full of plants has more material for thought in it than one who has not tried it can possibly imagine.   It is all healthy thought, too, unless the mind is very perverse or morbid; and throws a grace about the matter-of-fact cares of daily life, which, without some re-creative resource, are apt to make mind and body grow old before their time.

There is one common mistake to be avoided in the selection of plants for house culture; and that is getting too many, and taking them too indis-criminately. A few nice plants will afford you much more pleasure than many indifferent ones. Do not have more than you can accommodate without inconvenience, and take thoroughly good care of without their becoming troublesome. The attempt to possess too much of any thing dimin-ishes our enjoyment of it even more than the hav-ing less than we could conveniently use. The true enjoyment of anything depends upon its adaptation to our tastes, and the amount of mental recreation and development we get from it; and not upon its quantity, or its value in the estimation of the world.

FILIAL AND PARENTAL LOVE.

"Call no man your father upon the earth: for one is your
Father, which is in heaven."—WORDS OF THE LORD.

XVI.

FILIAL AND PARENTAL LOVE.

THAT the relationship existing between parent and child, as implying one ruling and the other ruled, belongs wholly to our temporal state, is a truth that must become apparent so soon as we reflect upon the eternal relation existing between every human being and the Heavenly Father. In the future life parent and child will doubtless seek each other and love each other, with an affection growing out of the love that bound them together here; but in the heavens, where all exist forever in the prime and perfection of adult life, a relationship, the essence of which is the result of difference in age, must naturally be lost, and those who were parents and children here must there become brothers and sisters, all filial and parental feeling being forgotten in a universal and childlike adoration of the one only Father.

Parents should bear this truth in mind, that it may modify the control they exercise over their children from the very beginning of their lives. Children should be controlled in order that they may learn to control themselves; guided, that they may learn to guide themselves. The parent should teach the child to feel that in obeying him he obeys the law of God; and as the child advances in years, he should be taught to seek in God's law for the guidance and control that he found in his parents at an earlier age.

Pride and love of dominion in the heart of the parent often make it very hard to give up parental authority, even after children become men and women; but the happiest, because the most heavenly, domestic relations can only be established where the filial and parental affections are gradually merged into a brotherly and sisterly love, no one seeking to command another, but all seeking to obey the Heavenly Father.

The ease with which parents control their children depends upon the degree in which they control themselves. A parent who is petulant, or irritable, or passionate, never can control a child with-

out a contest, because the child is never sure that
he shall be obliged to obey if he resist. Petulance
and ill-temper are childish weapons; and parents
who make use of them put themselves on a level
with their children, and have no true authority
over them. Self-control is a weapon a child cannot use, and the parent who is armed with it is
sure of an easy victory.

Self-control is not always a virtue, because it
may be the result of pride of character. When
this is the case, the parent may exercise a perfect
control over the child, but his power will be evil,
because he will endeavor to be as a god in his
own house, and instead of lifting the minds of his
children to the worship of the Heavenly Father,
he will try to fix them upon himself with an idol-
atrous reverence. Parents who take pride in the
obedience of their children never wish to give
up their power over them, and they sometimes
induce a pride of filial feeling in their children
that leads them to continue their obedience so
long as they live in this world. This is very
wrong on both sides; for the parent asks, and the
child gives, what of right belongs to the Lord.
Every adult person is responsible in the first and
highest degree to the Lord, and breaks the first

and greatest Commandment if he suffer his sense of right and wrong to be controlled by any human being. Idol worship cannot cease to be a sin, even though the idol be a parent.

More frequently pride of dominion in the parent, though it may control the child in early life, rouses opposition as he becomes older; and the most painful discord is the result of the attempt of the parent to retain what no longer of right belongs to him. Parents who are unwilling to acknowledge that their children are men and women when they become so, and who endeavor to keep from them the liberty wherewith the Lord makes all his children free, have no true conception of the parental office; and in striving to retain that which does not belong to them, they lose the affectionate respect which they might always enjoy, if they would but love their children as free human beings and not as property; as belonging not to them but to the Lord. Parents who are governed by pride and the love of dominion are apt to deceive themselves into the belief that their love for their children is truly parental; and if their children oppose them as they grow older, they feel themselves deeply wronged, and often become full of resentment towards them. The Scriptures tell us a mother may forget her child, but that the Lord will never forget us; and the indulgence of pride, and the love of rule, which is very sure to accompany pride, render a mother peculiarly liable to forget her maternal love. They only are true parents who cannot feel anger and resentment towards their children.

It is a very noticeable fact that a parent almost never turns away from a child who leads a bad life, a life of opposition to the law of God. When we hear that a parent has turned from his child, forgotten his parental feeling, we are almost sure to hear that the child has thwarted the parent's will. If he had opposed only the will of his Heavenly Father, his earthly father could have forgiven him; but opposition to his own will is an offence not to be overlooked.

I am inclined to believe that we may lay it down as an axiom, that it is never religious principle, but always pride, that holds dominion in a parent's heart when he turns away from his child.

To those in whom filial and parental affection are very strong, it may be a painful thought that these will be changed into friendship in the world to come; although there need be no diminution of the tenderness of affection on either side.

When, however, faith is changed to sight, we can now but faintly imagine the fulness of filial devotion with which we shall turn to the Lord. Herein must be infinite scope for the exercise of all that part of our nature that craves parental support; that delights to look up and worship; that seeks a returning love that cannot grow cold or forgetful.   For those too who find their greatest happiness in the exercise of parental care, there will be an endless joy afforded by the multitudes of little children daily and hourly passing away from earth, and ascending to the heavenly mansions.   These are all to be trained step by step in the other life as here, only with a certainty of perfect training there that cannot be insured here. Every child who passes away from this world, as it leaves its mother's arms, is received " by angels who are of the female sex, who in the life of the body tenderly loved infants, and at the same time loved God," and who are of a character precisely adapted to meet the wants of these children of their adoption, and to educate them into angelic life.   Thus parental love will find an endless field for exercise, and will live on through the coming ages; for heaven can never become full, and earth

never cease to swell the tide of life that flows onward from time to eternity.

If parents would but awake to a distinct conviction that the children born to them are not
absolutely their own, but only intrusted to them
by the Lord, in order that they may receive their
first lessons in an education that, if rightly begun
here, will go on unfolding and expanding through
all eternity into a heavenly life, the progress
of which will never end, it seems to me that they
would feel an irresistible incentive to strive to the
utmost of their ability to bring up their children
rightly, and to seek from the Lord the instruction
which He alone can give to guide them in their
endeavors.

There is an appalling ignorance and misconcep-
tion of Scripture, and want of faith in the efficacy
of prayer, in a large proportion of this so-called
Christian community, that make Christian life an
impossibility; and without this there can be no
true education, no leading out of those higher
faculties of man which lift him above the brute.

In order to educate your children, you must
first be educated yourself; and you should examine yourself to ascertain how well you are prepared for your office of teacher. You may train

them into all worldly wisdom by means of the instruction the world will give you; but if you believe in a future life, and that there is a connection between that and the present, you must feel desirous that your children should be prepared to enter upon it with a reasonable hope of happiness. The world can give you no information in regard to a preparation for heaven. It can teach you to lay up all manner of earthly treasure, but it is dumb when you interrogate it concerning heavenly things.

God and the Bible are the only sources whence positive truth can come to humanity; and they only are truly educated who have learned how to obtain the truth from these sources. It will not do to confine the reading of Scripture to Sunday, or to days when you have leisure. It must be daily food to you if you would have a symmetrical growth to your spiritual nature. The soul depends on daily food as much as the body, in order to become healthy and strong. You cannot comprehend the Scriptures if you only read them now and then. They yield their wisdom only to those who seek to make them the daily law of their lives, and who come to them reverently and pray-

erfully, believing them to be the veritable Word
of God.

More directly still we may obtain heavenly
truth from the Heavenly Father himself, in answer to our prayers, if we will pray to Him as
children pray, believing that He is our personal
friend, ready to help us through every doubt and
emergency, to strengthen us in all weakness and
trial, to give unto us whatever we ask in devout
faith.

God's Word and prayer to Him are as needful
to one who would lead a Christian life, as the
compass and the observations of the heavenly
bodies are to the mariner. We should all condemn the folly of a shipmaster, who let his vessel
sail on without daily observations of his latitude
and longitude; but if we begin a day without
looking for aid to our Heavenly Father, we drift
through our affairs just as foolishly. Rocks and
quicksands are all about us, and we are liable to
mistakes at every moment. Unless the spiritual
sun is shining into our souls we are walking in
darkness, and we have no reason to expect to receive its light unless we open our hearts to it by
prayer. We must ask before we receive; we

must seek before we shall find; we must knock before the heavenly door will be opened to us.

I suppose there is no duty in life more difficult to perform rightly than the training of children, and no parent has any right to hope for success unless he uses every means that the Divine Providence affords. The Lord tells us: "I am the light of the world: he that followeth me shall not walk in darkness, but shall have the light of life." There is no light for the soul but that which cometh from Him; but unless the soul turns itself towards Him it cannot receive His light, though it shines perpetually with abounding fulness. It forces itself upon no one, and we cannot perceive it until we feel that we are wandering in darkness, and voluntarily seek after it. No day is wisely begun that does not begin with prayer, and when moments come throughout the day in which we are perplexed with doubt as to which way our duty lies, or troubled with temptation to do that which is wrong, or to refrain from doing that which is right, momentary aspiration heavenward will instruct us, and strengthen us better than all that the world or our own souls can tell us. Could we but remember this at all times we might lead heavenly lives while yet dwelling upon earth;

but the world and our own self-love too often blind our eyes to heavenly visions, stop our ears to heavenly voices, and make us forget their existence when we stand most in need of their aid. Through them alone our spiritual natures can become educated, and through them alone can we learn how to meet the daily exigencies that arise in the training of children. The ear of the Lord is ever open to our questionings. Let us strive not to forget to ask of Him all that we need.

DISAPPOINTMENTS.

"Blessed is the man whose strength is in thee; who passing through the valley of misery maketh of it a well."—PSALMS OF DAVID.

XVII.

DISAPPOINTMENTS.

ITHERTO I have said little of the disappointments of a garden, yet they are not unfrequent, scattered among its many pleasures. The frosts of winter and the droughts of summer are often fatal to plants; while their roots, stalks, leaves, and blossoms, each have their peculiar enemies among the worm and insect tribes; sometimes working insidiously beneath the ground or within the bark, and sometimes infesting leaf and blossom with their disgusting forms, which are rendered the more revolting by the beauty of the objects they destroy. Sometimes plants perish without any apparent cause, perhaps from some natural defect in themselves that incapacitates them from being nourished into a healthy growth. Then too our own ignorance or indolence, carelessness or forgetfulness, often stand in the way of our success in the garden, as in all other departments of life.

Were it not for this liability to disappointment the garden would offer but a very imperfect correspondence to human life; for there uncertainty hangs over all things. Many, and indeed most disappointments in life, as well as in the garden, are the direct consequence of our own shortcomings in the fulfilment of our duties; but there are others which come from causes we cannot foresee nor control, which the natural man hates as the work of chance; but before which the spiritual man bows in humble submission, for the voice within his soul says: "Be still, and know that I am God."

When we fail in our endeavors we should be careful to ascertain if some neglect of our own is not the cause of what we suffer. In our unwillingness to criminate ourselves, we may call that a dispensation of Providence which is the direct result of our own misconduct; and unless we acknowledge this honestly, we shall be liable to a life of disappointment. It is generally quite easy for us to understand why our neighbor does not succeed in his undertakings; and if we would but silence the pratings of self-love, we might as easily comprehend our own failures.

If we procure roots and seeds, and place them in our gardens without knowing anything of the habits of the plants that are to come from them, we must look forward to probable failure in their growth; yet it is no uncommon thing to see men and women, in the daily walks of life, setting causes at work with just as little regard to consequences; as it were sowing seeds at random, and then complaining that things do not come up right;—sowing dog-wood and ivy, and wondering that they will come up poisonous; scattering the seeds of all manner of ill-named plants, and then complaining that their ground is full of weeds.

Ignorance is one reason for all this, but it is not an excuse; because we have no right to work ignorantly. Want of thought is another reason; but neither have we a right to be thoughtless.

An unsuccessful life sometimes appears to be the result of mental incompetency; but if we look a little closer we are pretty sure to find that this incompetency is moral, and that a better morality would have obviated it. Pride, vanity, self-indulgence, ignorance, thoughtlessness, and indolence are the immoralities that are perpetually bringing failure to the endeavors of those who are their slaves; and it is seldom we can find failure apart from one or another of them.

When disappointment comes to us, do not let us fold our hands and call it a dark Providence until we have catechised our own hearts honestly with such questions as these :—

Did vanity induce me to attempt something I might have known was beyond my ability to reach? Did pride make me .unwilling to do all that I should to attain my purpose, or prevent me from seeking information from others as to the means of attaining it? Did self-indulgence lead me to spend extravagantly the property or the time that should have been used in my business, or indolence prevent my making a due application of it? Did the desire of shining in the eyes of my neighbors lead me to live beyond my income, and incur debts that I had no reason to expect I should be able to pay?

It is not often that failure in endeavors after worldly success comes to us if we can answer all questions involving our own fault in the negative. In fact, failure in social life, with no moral cause by which it may be accounted for, is as rare as failure in gardening with no apparent physical cause. If we choose a situation in a good soil, and plant and cultivate with such knowledge as we may readily attain if we will, we can hardly fail to have a fine garden ; and even a poor soil may with patience and skilful industry be made to produce some kinds of plants and fruits quite worth the pains. So in all positions of life, if we will but work with determined industry, and spend with conscientious economy, it must be some extra-ordinary cause that prevents our success ; and if we fail for a while, we are almost sure to succeed at last.

In speaking of spending with conscientious economy, I do not wish to be understood as meaning spending money alone. Strength both of mind and body, eye-sight, and every power and means of effort and of use that we possess, we may squander uselessly, or in vain and impatient endeavors after too speedy a success. Health and strength of body and of mind are the two choicest gifts we can inherit, and if we waste them we are more foolish and more reprehensible than they who throw away external wealth ; because that may be regained, while impaired faculties can never be restored to their original vigor. Moreover, the waste of any power or means, even though it be recovered, involves a waste of time that can never be recovered. Time lost is lost forever, and the greatness of the loss is something we cannot measure. The gifts of God are many and various, and happy are we if we use them, whatever they may be, remembering that they are His gifts; and that whether we have one talent or ten intrusted to our keeping, we are alike responsible to Him, each in our proportion, for the manner in which we employ them.

To meet disappointments, that come to us we know not from what cause, or to what end, with a serene faith in the wisdom and love of our Heavenly Father, is one of our most important, and often one of our most difficult duties. Human pride wishes to understand all things, and to subdue all things to its will; and when it finds itself entangled and overcome in a web of circumstance that it can neither comprehend nor control, it is wounded to its inmost depths, and feels itself unkindly and unjustly dealt by.

While we are successful in our undertakings, and all goes well with us, we are apt to be content with ourselves, and to suppose we are leading very good lives, and we offer our thanksgivings and prayers to heaven in a joyful spirit, running, as it were, to meet the Lord, like the young man who had great possessions. The Lord looks upon us with a clearer vision than our own, and sees that we lack that love for Him which would make us feel that all we have is His and not our own, and He tells us this by taking from us something we highly prize; wealth or health, child or friend. Instead of perceiving and worshipping the Infinite Mercy, we turn away sorrowing, for we had deemed our possessions our own; and pride so blinds our eyes that we are incapable of seeing why we should be called upon to give them up.

The implicit obedience which a wise parent requires of a young child, is the counterpart of the submission which we owe to our Heavenly Father. Spiritually we are but children so long as we remain in this world. We are often as unable to comprehend why our Heavenly Father denies our wishes, as a baby is why his mother will not suffer him to put his hands into the pretty flame of the lamp he grasps after so eagerly. Painful experience soon teaches the child that wisdom and love came between him and his desires; and so we, if we make any advances in spiritual growth, can look back and comprehend many things which were quite dark to us when they took place.

Discipline is always painful to us while we are suffering it, just in proportion as it is needful to us; and it is not until we have reached a plane above it that we can fully comprehend it. The early growth of every good principle planted in the soul is dark and secret, like the sprouting of seed in the earth, and it is only He who plants who knows what should come of it. If we submit ourselves in faithful love to the culture of the Heavenly Gardener, we shall gradually discover the result of His work in the development of traits of character that will be a perpetual source of peace and joy to us.

A child who has been brought up by religious parents in the habit of implicit obedience, has received from them the best possible preparation for meeting the disappointments of life with calm and patient trust in the parental providence of God; and this is the surest foundation on which human happiness can be built. We sometimes hear parents say that they will indulge their children in everything they can, because care and disappointment will come fast enough as they grow up; but such indulgence in early life makes care and disappointment doubly hard to bear when they come. A child whose wilfulness and selfishness and in-

dolence are indulged is never happy in childhood; and when he grows up and finds his plans
and wishes thwarted by a power he cannot with-
stand, and whose wisdom and mercy he is incom-
petent to comprehend, he "kicks against the
pricks" in impotent rage or despair, having no
staff to support him under the chastisement of the
Divine rod. Trusting obedience to the earthly
parent is a germ that naturally and easily unfolds
and expands into an obedient and loving faith in
the Heavenly Parent; and that is the only never-
failing support in the hour of trial and disappointment.

DROUGHT.

"My doctrine shall drop as the rain, my speech shall distil as the dew, as the small rain upon the tender herb, and as the showers upon the grass."—DEUTERONOMY.

XVIII.

DROUGHT.

DURING the past spring our neighborhood suffered from a drought of such severity as occurs not more than once in a long series of years. The air was so dry and parched that it could not give its usual refreshment to the lungs, and the earth lacked moisture to feed the roots of the vegetable world.

My garden, instead of luring me out in the pleasant days of April, as it has done in previous years, repelled me by its aridness; and I found so little pleasure in doing what seemed absolutely essential for its preservation, that it was difficult for me to remember that hitherto all I had done there had been a labor of love.

Such seasons, though poor in what we love to seek after, are rich in instruction; and though

(221)

natural fruits may be denied us, spiritual ones are
always to be found.

A period of drought in the natural world corresponds to the periods in our spiritual experience
when we lack heavenly truth to support the wants
of the soul ; when our spiritual bodies are parched
and feverish, and we have not strength to bear the
heat of the Divine Love.   The Divine Love shines
always upon us, just as the sun shines always
upon the earth ; but unless its heat is tempered by
clouds and rain it becomes distressing, and seems
baneful rather than beneficent.

The soul that has made little or no progress in
the regenerate life cannot feel that the Divine
Providence is always full of tenderness and mercy
in its dealings with mankind.   It writhes under
the bereavements and disappointments of life, like
an infant undergoing some surgical operation when
it is too young to have any comprehension of its
necessity.   The parents look on and weep at the
suffering of the child, but pray the surgeon to go
on in spite of its cries ; for they can understand
that some future good is to follow, so essential to
the child's health or life that the present pain is
not to be weighed against it for a moment.   So
the angels, if they are aware of our mental suffer-

ing under the knife of the Divine Surgeon, would not ask him to stay His hand; for they would perceive the disease from which he was striving to deliver us, and would beg us to yield ourselves confidingly to His efforts in our behalf, that we might be made whole.

The water and the mineral substances which plants take up through their roots out of the earth, correspond to natural truth and goodness. The light and heat which come down to them from the sun, correspond to spiritual truth and goodness. These four aliments, in due proportion, are all essential to the complete development of the plant; and if either becomes excessive, or is diminished, so as to lose its proportion with the rest, the plant suffers, and perhaps dies.

The human soul is just as dependent for its regenerate life and growth upon natural and spiritual goodness and truth as the plant is upon the varieties of sustenance it derives from earth and sky.

Natural truth and goodness guide and support us in all the duties of life that relate to natural things. They make us faithful in the performance of all that relates to the professions, trades, and daily external duties of every kind that belong to life in this world. Spiritual truth and goodness guide and support us in the duties that belong to the internal life, bringing the thoughts and affections into harmony with the Divine Law, so that we not only do our duty, but love to do it; because we feel that inasmuch as we are faithful in the performance of all the daily charities of life towards our fellow-beings, we are doing them unto the Lord, and so coming day by day nearer to Him.

A plant may grow quite rankly into foliage under a clouded sky, sustained by a much larger proportion of water and of minerals than of light and heat; but in order to produce blossoms and fruits, which is the essential object of a plant, light and heat must come from above in due proportion to the nutriment its roots suck up from below; while, at the same time, the plant never requires so large a quantity of what it draws from the earth as when it is lifting its crowning graces of flowers and fruits towards heaven. Herein* is involved a very important correspondence, teaching a truth but little understood in the world at large.

It is quite a common idea that spiritual life lifts us out of and above material and natural life; instead of which, the more spiritualized we become, the better we appreciate the value of the natural life, and the more faithful we become in the discharge of our material duties. A human being can no more rise above the duties of the natural life than a plant can rise above drawing up nutriment through its roots. One who tries to lead a spiritual life apart from the world, and without recognizing the social duties, is like a cut flower in a vase of water, which, though it may retain its beauty for many days, can never perfect its fruit.

Whenever the dispensations of Providence are contrary to our wishes, and we are not able to comprehend them, we suffer spiritual drought. The love of our Heavenly Father is invariable; and He is constantly doing all that He can, without infringing upon our liberty, to draw us to Himself. We are not always able to receive the dispensations of His love, because we have not truth enough in our minds to comprehend that it is love. So long as the desires of our hearts are satisfied, we feel that His love is blessing us, and we rejoice in the warmth of the Heavenly Sun; but when His love denies us our desires, and bereaves us of our possessions, if we cannot perceive the wisdom and mercy of the dispensation, we no longer feel that the heavenly sun sheds a grateful warmth upon us, for it seems like a "consuming fire." Then the soul is parched with drought, and its good affections and true thoughts languish and wither; but they do not perish entirely if we have any remains of genuine faith in the Lord within our souls. Such remnants of faith are like the moisture stored up in the earth, which is made to rise by the heat of the soil when it is parched in the sunshine. The more carefully the soil of the garden is cultivated during a drought the easier it is for the heat of the sun to penetrate it, and to bring the hidden moisture upward to the roots of the plants. So when we are most severely tried by spiritual drought we suffer much less if we go on doing our duty faithfully in all the external details of life, and weed out evil affections and irreverent thoughts as they spring up, and threaten to choke the better growth of the mind. If we neglect our duties, our hearts become hardened so that the rays of the Divine Love cannot penetrate them, and the roots of our good affections find no moisture to feed upon. Then, too, the more carefully we keep our hearts tender by striving to do our duty towards every one around us, the better prepared we shall be to receive fresh supplies of the Divine

Truth; just as a soil mellowed by constant culture drinks in the falling rain readily, while it is shed off if the soil has been suffered to lie baking in the sun till a hard crust is formed upon it. Selfish repining, that dwells morbidly upon its own griefs, neglecting, or forgetting, to open its heart towards the neighbor in the daily charities of life, forms just such a hardened crust about the soul, impenetrable to the Divine Truth that strives to bless it by telling it what it should do to be saved.

There is no form in which water falls from heaven to earth which is not used in the Scriptures to illustrate the coming down of Heavenly Doctrine to the soul. It "comes down like rain upon the mown grass; as showers that water the earth." It comes in "a plentiful rain to confirm the inheritance of the Lord when it is weary." It "distils as the dew" and drops "as the small rain upon the tender herb." "As the rain cometh down, and the snow from heaven, and returneth not thither, but watereth the earth, and maketh it bring forth and bud, that it may give seed to the sower, and bread to the eater: so shall my word be that goeth forth out of my mouth."

Varying as the states of the human beings to whom it is addressed, it modifies itself to our necessities, not waiting for us to seek it, but striving ever to approach in some form that we may be willing to open our hearts and receive when it stands and knocks at our door. How mean and pitiful is the pride of man when we compare it with the infinite humility of the Lord. We never sink so low that His love does not follow us. We never make our hearts so hard that His truth does not strive to penetrate them. Even when frost-bound, in the very winter of faithlessness, His truth falls about us like the snow, and waits till the influence of some good affection softens our hearts with its spring-like warmth; and then, gently dissolving, it sinks into the soil, making it "bring forth and bud, that it may give seed to the sower and bread to the eater."

While we remain in this world we must not expect to arrive at a spiritual perfection that will carry us beyond the changes of state that correspond to the different seasons of the year, with their variations of heat and cold, drought and moisture. Human progress is never steadily upward, never unwaveringly onward, towards the heavenly goal. The loves of self and of the world never die out entirely even in the best; and so often as we yield to their allurements we forget the Lord and the neighbor, thinking only how we may follow out the devices of our own hearts. But we can never find peace or rest while we are thus led astray, unless pride and selfishness become so entirely dominant in our souls as to suffocate our capacity for distinguishing between right and wrong, truth and falsehood. The image and likeness of God into which the spiritual body of the human race was originally created, though defaced and broken in our fallen natures, still mourns and laments within us, asserting its claim to be restored to its integrity; and we can never escape from its complaints unless we banish every heavenly aspiration from our souls. Accordingly as we resist or yield ourselves to these aspirations our pilgrimage is through drought, and coldness, and sterility, or through softly-falling rain, and grateful sunshine, and fertile fields.

As the manner in which the earth inclines itself towards the sun, and the condition of its garment of atmosphere, decide in what form moisture shall fall upon its surface, so our states and spheres decide whether the Divine Truth shall be presented to us with a harshness corresponding to hail, or snow, or tempest, or whether it shall come like the gentle dew or the softly-falling rain. Happy are we if we recognize and accept it when it comes, be its form or its medium what it may !

INSECTS AND WORMS.

Noxious insects and worms are to the garden what sensuous falsities are to the spiritual life : small and unimportant as they may seem, they are possessed of a fearful power to destroy.

XIX.

INSECTS AND WORMS.

THERE are no disappointments connected with garden culture that are more hard to bear than those which we suffer through the depredations of insects and of worms. We often observe some thrifty young plant wilting without any apparent cause. If we touch it it falls into the hand, and we find that it has been cut off just below the surface of the earth; and on opening the earth we find a large white worm who has done the mischief. Many seedlings are devoured by insects as soon as their leaves are formed, and others suffer in foliage and flowers at a later period. Insects so small that one can hardly imagine them capable of doing much harm, yet come in such numbers as to prove a pest over a whole garden. The more highly we cultivate, the more varied and numerous these enemies become, and the choicest flowers and the most delicate fruits are those which are most attractive to them. To conquer them requires unwearying watchfulness and perseverance, and some of them can hardly be overcome even by these.

Repulsive and annoying as these creatures are, they have a lesson for us which we shall do well to learn and lay to heart; for, like all other creatures, they exist because they correspond to things within us, and we should struggle to cast these out with far more earnestness than we strive to banish insects from our gardens.

All winged creatures correspond to thoughts or perceptions; and, unwilling as we may be to believe it, we all of us have thoughts which are represented for our instruction in the disgusting insect no less than in the beautifully painted butterfly or the graceful bird.

The flight of birds and insects corresponds to the movement of our thoughts; and we may readily perceive many illustrations of this as we watch the motions of the common frequenters of our gardens.

There are birds of long and rapid flight, like those swift thoughts that sweep the universe and scan the whole creation. Birds of strong and heavy flight, like thoughts that build up arguments, and wall themselves around what we accept as truth. Birds rapid and combative, flying like the thoughts that contend in argument, and often torment the stouter enemy although they may not overcome him. Birds such as the friendly robin, so tame as to be almost domestic, flying but short distances, and remaining near the same spot all the year around, hibernating in hollow trees and snug corners, resembling the thoughts that belong to our domestic duties and daily cares ; quiet, unexciting thoughts, that build up our homes by forming the domestic virtues. And there are birds that scale the atmosphere, singing as they rise, until they pass beyond human sight and hearing, like the adoring thoughts that contemplate the Divine perfections.

Wings correspond to spiritual truths. They are the powers by which birds and insects lift themselves upward, just as spiritual truths lift up our thoughts towards heaven.

All things can be perverted, and we are prone to turn to evil that which was created good. Our thoughts do not always move on wings of spiritual truth. Too often we make to ourselves wings of falsehood, and it seems to us that they give us power to rise with a bolder and freer flight than the others. Not that we acknowledge to ourselves that they are of falsehood; but that we, through looking to ourselves instead of to the Lord, as the source whence we may draw the truth, distort and pervert it, or else lose ourselves in total error. When we try to see by our own light, we lose the power of seeing by the light which cometh down from heaven, and flutter hither and thither with uncertain flight, having no sun to direct our course. Then our thoughts correspond to unclean birds and noxious insects, and worms which are insects in their rudimentary states; and they devour the truths we may hold in our memories, perverting them into their own forms, just as those creatures consume and fatten upon the produce of our gardens. If the mind becomes wholly immersed in falsities it is like a region overspread with locusts, that leave neither fruit, flower, nor foliage undestroyed.

We sometimes hear a spiritual truth that we receive with satisfaction, and it takes root and grows like a healthy plant; but perhaps it is an inconvenient truth that lies in the way of the gratification of some selfish desire hidden within our hearts so deeply that we are hardly aware of its existence.

Every evil desire is married to a lie that is ready to assert, so often as we will listen, that its mate is good, and that we are fools if we will not indulge it. If we listen long this lie will bite off the root of the opposing truth, and it will wilt away and die, and an evil weed of falsehood will presently flourish in its place.

It is a noteworthy fact, that worms do not eat up weeds. The hand of the gardener must remove them. Things poisonous and things useless flourish freely; but things which serve for food and for the delight of the eyes the worm is always waiting to devour.

The slug which has been introduced to our gardens upon the perpetual roses, is an excessively destructive enemy, often making that disgusting which would otherwise be the most beautiful of all our flowering plants. So society in its most refined state is probably most full of all manner of falsehoods, making for itself a code of conventionalisms which it puts in place of all moral and religious law, till it is as bare of spiritual truth as a rose-bed is bare of greenness when the slug has been left to work out its will. In spite of this destruction to the leaves, the roses bloom for several seasons, though the life of the plant is eventually overcome by it; and in this we may see a correspondence to those persons who make themselves attractive in society by the grace and elegance of their manners, but in whom all the truths that are stored up in childhood, or which are presented to them from time to time in later life, are destroyed by the sensuous falsities of fashion, that perpetually put that which belongs only to the externals of life, above that which must remain with us forever.

The rose-bugs that devour the blossoms but do not touch the leaves, may be compared to those falsities which destroy all that is graceful in life, basing all ideas of wisdom on a bare and frigid utilitarianism. The utilitarian has no idea of good beyond material wealth ministering to the physical wants of humanity; and his whole plan of culture, intellectual and moral, is based on a desire for the attainment of happiness in this world. All that leads to purely moral or intellectual happiness, apart from material possession, is to him futile and visionary. Flowers have no place in his garden, and the fig-tree should be his favorite plant, because it bears fruit without apparently blossoming. To him it must be an unintelligible mystery that the All-Wise has created so many plants that finish their work, so far as we are concerned, when they expand their flowers. To be sure, the seeds of such plants may feed a great many birds; but then most birds are as useless as flowers.

We are apt to feel that refinement and culture must be inherently good, and that persons surrounded by elegance and luxury are shielded from temptation to evil far more than those who dwell amid poverty and ignorance. Yet in truth no class of human beings are in greater danger of putting truth for falsehood and falsehood for truth, than those who dwell at ease amid the luxuries of wealth. The senses are so constartly ministered to in the refined life of the present day, that it requires no small amount of determination to avoid becoming completely enslaved by them. The eye and ear, the touch and taste and smell, are all pampered to the utmost by the luxurious appointments of modern civilization, till their wants often become paramount to all others, and a refined sensualism becomes the highest good to which the soul aspires. Out of this sensualism a whole code of laws is evolved, upon which the morality of society is based, without regard to the absolute and eternal laws of right and wrong, which have been sent down from heaven for our guidance. The falsities of this code, like the slugs in our rose-beds, cling upon every thought of the mind, destroying all truth, till nothing but bare forms without life remain. The skeletons, in the shape of leaves, but incapable of performing any of their functions, that deface the beauty of our gardens, are no more useless to the plant than the semblances of truth are to the mind, which cling about it when it has become enslaved to the senses.

Sap rises in a plant in a crude state, and is of no use until it passes into the leaves, and becomes elaborated there into something that can nourish vegetable growth, and perfect the fruit; just as in the bodies of animals the blood must be elaborated in the lungs before it can nourish the system. Truth is to the mind what blood is to the body, or sap to the plant; but it must go through a process of elaboration by rational thought in the understanding, before it can promote the mind's growth. The understanding is to the mind what the lungs are to the body, or the foliage to plants. If the understanding is filled with falsities the truth cannot abide there, but is driven out or perverted, so that the mind can gain no healthful growth. Our highly cultivated gardens breed worms and insects no faster than the fastidious re-

finement and luxurious self-indulgences of elegant
society breed falsities ; and spiritual life is nowhere
in greater danger than where the appliances of
material life are most abounding.

These sensuous falsities will tell us that refinement of feeling is commensurate with refinement of
external life ; that persons who live poorly think and
feel coarsely, and are incapable of refined enjoyment or of tender affection ; and if we believe all
this, our hearts will be closed against the sufferings
of the larger part of our fellow beings, and we
shall be indulgent to ourselves and indifferent to
them, just in proportion to the degree of faith we
give to this falsehood. Again, the fallacies of the
senses may tell us that refinement of feeling is always accompanied by refinement of manner, and
may lead us to a fastidiousness of culture in this
direction that will shut out from our sympathies
all who, from ignorance or carelessness, do not
submit themselves to the same laws of courtesy,
or elegance, or etiquette, which we choose to adopt
as our standard. Refined society often condemns
awkwardness of manner or bluntness of remark,
as greater sins than impurity of life, and refuses
its favors to those on whom fashion does not set its
seal. Christian truth enlarges the heart and

widens the sympathies, while worldly fallacies make the heart that feeds upon them narrower and colder day by day.

Sensualism is not, however, confined to refined society, any more than worms and insects are confined to flower-gardens. I have dwelt upon it there, because, to many persons, it does not seem to occur that there may be just as much of it in elegance as there is in coarseness; and because it seems to me that self-asserting fastidiousness of manner and conversation rarely has any other foundation than sensualism. Christian charity pervading the character gives to it a genuine refinement that always respects the rights of others, and never puts forth its own claim to homage or observation. The fastidiousness of sensualism loves to display its fancied superiority by self-assertion, and by criticisms upon others; and this often in a way so unfeeling, as to show a total want of that genuine Christian refinement that never inflicts a wanton wound. Fastidiousness in manners, like spiritual pride in morals, draws all its life from the love of self and of the world; while true refinement, like true morality, is the outward form of love to the neighbor, purified and instructed by love to the Lord. It is very easy for every one to perceive that a drunkard or a glutton is given up to sensualism; but this vice in its refinement is not so apparent as in its coarseness. The one is, however, no less fatal to spiritual growth than the other. We may lead what the world calls a faultless life, and yet be wholly immersed in sensualism. We may have what the world calls perfect taste in art, in literature, in manners, and yet never have a thought or feeling that rises above the plane of sensualism.

The sensualism of poverty has but few ways of showing itself, and so is manifested with a violence that shocks us at once by its coarseness. Every advance we make towards wealth opens new modes of sensual enjoyment to us, and thus diminishes the apparent strength of our sensualism, by spreading it over a wider surface. We are disgusted as we meet a poor creature in the street, reeking with tobacco and spirits, and are full of wonder that he will spend so much of his earnings in such coarse indulgence of his senses; and yet perhaps the power of spreading a luxurious table for ourselves is all that saves us from just such coarseness, and we are perhaps as extravagant in this as he whom we condemn. So fast as we become possessed of the means, we almost all of us lavish all that we

can afford, and sometimes much more than we can
afford, on fine clothes, fine houses, fine furniture,
delicate food, pictures, statues, plate, horses and
carriages, and all for the gratification of the senses;
and then we lift up our hands in horror at the
poor who indulge their senses in the only way
their means permit.   And those who indulge
themselves most lavishly, are usually the loudest
in condemning the want of self-control in others.

There is nothing wrong in loving beautiful
things, or in seeking to possess them, for the senses
were given us for enjoyment as well as for instruction.   The sin lies in making enjoyment first, and
paramount to, the instruction and the use; and perhaps even in forgetting everything but enjoyment;
resting, like the brutes that perish, in the now,
without thinking of the hereafter, which must be
the result of the now.

So far as the enjoyments of luxury make us indifferent to our duties as human beings, accountable to our Heavenly Father for the use we make
of His beneficence, we are resting in the sensualism of luxury.   So far as the possession of luxury
inflates our pride and vanity, we extinguish our
intellectual and moral perceptions, and measure
all things by a sensual standard.   The things

which we perceive through the means of our senses are intended to form a basis upon which the things of intellectual and moral perception are to be built up. If we rest contentedly on that plane of development which belongs to the senses, we invert the order of our being, putting the intellectual and the moral below the sensual; for we always make that which is least developed in our minds subservient to that which is more so.

Whenever our love for music, for art, or for luxury in any of its forms, overpowers our judgment or our morality, making us extravagant in acquisition, or selfish in enjoyment, it is because our love is sensuous, and we are becoming enslaved by the lusts of the eye or the ear, or by the pride of life. Purified from what is selfish and worldly, the enjoyments that come to us through the senses lead us upward to the highest spirituality. Not by destroying the senses, but by regenerating them, are we to be reformed into the Divine image.

Some insects lay their eggs in the heart of the blossoms of fruit-bearing trees, and as the fruit grows the worm hatches, and eats its way into the outer world through the food that surrounds it. The more delicate fruits are entirely destroyed by this means; but apples and pears thus infested ripen by some morbid process sooner than they otherwise would, and drop from the tree, giving us what we call windfalls. These, though inferior in quality to those which remain their proper time upon the tree, serve us usefully until we can get that which is better. Fruits correspond to good works; blossoms, to the the aspirations of the mind when it has received the truth, and is desiring to bring it out into good works. The worm that is born in the blossom represents a falsity that comes into the mind in connection with a truth, sometimes stimulating it to good works from bad motives.

We seldom act from entirely true or entirely false principles. The true and the false sometimes struggle within us for the mastery, and sometimes act so harmoniously that we are not aware, unless we examine our hearts very carefully, that we are actuated by anything but the truth. Pride and vanity and selfishness are worms continually coming to life within the better aspirations of the mind, and stimulating it to an activity that makes us eager to do seemingly good works; works wherein zeal runs before knowledge, and consequences are disregarded as unworthy of consideration. Such works are but windfalls of the mind, and not its ripened fruits. The works which are done from love to the neighbor, founded upon love to the Lord, are like fair, full-grown fruits, ripened duly by sun and shower. Works seemingly good, but which derive their impulse wholly or in part from the love of self and of the world, are like fruits full of gnarls and imperfections, occasioned by the secret enemy within, winding his crooked way through the flesh, and producing premature falling from the tree and speedy decay.

Whenever we are wrathful or regardless of consequences in the doing of what we call good works, we may be sure that the worm of self-love is at work in our hearts, and that what we are calling philanthropy, or charity, or any other good name, is only a form of the love of doing our own will. If we have an impetuous temper, which we acknowledge should not be indulged indiscriminately, we find perhaps great relief, and even a kind of self-satisfaction, in indulging it in what we consider a discriminating way, upon those who differ from us in politics, in religion, or in matters of social reform. We perhaps condemn our neighbor with the utmost virulence on such grounds, calling our intemperate wrath righteous indignation, or holy hatred; and do not seem to think we thereby tarnish the purity of our philanthropy, our patriotism, or our piety. The Almighty makes even "the wrath of man to praise Him;" over-ruling and restraining it till He can bend its effects to His own wise and loving purposes; but this does not make our indulgence of it the less per-nicious to our own souls. Offences must come, but this does not diminish the woe to those by whom they come. Philanthropy that measures the depth of its love for its favorites by the violence of its hatred towards the rest of society, has no better foundation than the love of its own self-will; and religion that cannot believe there is any way of salvation but the one in which itself walks, is based upon a self-asserting spiritual pride. The wind-fall works that are born of fanatical zeal, are dis-credited in the great harvest of the ages, while the ripened results that come from the calm self-control of true piety and charity go on blessing the world in ever-widening results from century to century.

We all know that the poor have claims upon us; but to aid the poor in such a way as will really benefit them, requires time, and care, and thought. Our indolence makes us unwilling to give these, and tells us that it is better to aid nine worthless objects than to let one worthy object go empty away; and we are thus often led to scatter our means indiscriminately, without reflecting that each unworthily bestowed alms takes from us just so much power of worthy benefaction; and that while we pay premiums to vice, we cannot, by just so much, do justice to virtue. This windfall charity is better for us than to shut our hearts against the calls of suffering, whether seeming or real; but we should not close our eyes to the fact that the worm of indolence is preventing the ripening of a far better fruit. A discriminating charity strengthens the hands of the poor to help themselves, while the indiscriminate giving of alms only makes the poor poorer, by teaching them to look to others for that which their own industry should provide.

In domestic life we are liable to fall into similar errors, through an impatient zeal that others should do what seems right in our eyes, or through an indolence that leads us to indulge the vices and foibles of those under our care or influence, rather than to take the trouble to curb them in their beginnings. A patience that is wise and yet earnest, that hastens not and yet rests not, ripens the domestic virtues into fulness of beauty, making home the type of heaven; but how seldom do we see this; how hard is it for us to do our part in forming such a home.

We are at the best short-sighted and fallible creatures, liable to err at every step; and knowing this, we should walk humbly with our fellows, not presuming to judge them as He who reads the heart alone can. Let us keep our judgments for our own works, and strive not to imagine them fair and beautiful while they are limited by our indolence, or sullied and alloyed by selfishness and pride. Let us remember that there is an eternal world, in which the worm dieth not; and let us hasten to cast it from us, and trample it under our feet, while we abide in the world of things that can be made to pass away.

THE POWER

AND

USE OF CIRCUMSTANCE.

"Every form changes to its own quality whatever flows into it."—SWEDENBORG.

"Where the bee sucks honey the spider sucks poison."

PROVERB.

XX.

THE POWER AND USE OF CIRCUMSTANCE.

THE garden teaches us innumerable lessons in its many forms of use and of beauty, and varied as these forms are, even so varied are the sermons they preach to those who willingly and reverently seek for instruction. There is, however, one great lesson which, though taught by the whole creation, is expressed more emphatically and more clearly in the garden than elsewhere, because there, more than anywhere else, a greater variety of forms is brought under the influence of similar circumstances. This lesson is, that circumstance has no power to create anything, nor even any part of anything; and that its power of modifying things after they are created, is limited by the innate peculiarities of those things.

Cultivation develops latent powers and characteristics in all things, but it gives them no new properties or parts. By enriching the juices of the plant it changes a worthless into a delicious fruit; turns leaf-buds into flower-buds, thereby increasing the quantity of fruit; and it may go still farther, by developing stamens and pistils into petals, till it destroys the fruit-producing power in the blossom. All this is but development, not creation. The plant-stems are full of latent leaf-germs, which appropriate nourishment develops into a branch, a leaf, or a blossom, which is but a cluster of leaves; for science teaches us that petal, pistil, and stamen, each result from the same kind of germ that produces a leaf, and that the difference in form and hue is the result of circumstance and not of innate peculiarity.

When we see how much may be done by culture in improving plants, we are liable to exaggerate our ideas of its power, and to feel as if it were almost, if not quite, creative. Still we cannot, through its means, change the absolute characteristics of anything. No amount of culture overcomes the poisonous qualities of a plant, and no neglect can make an innocent plant poisonous. Unless the germ of goodness was originally formed in the plant, no labor of ours can develop anything good; and if its original germ was evil, we labor in vain to subdue it except by total destruction.

The human mind is as a garden, and its various traits are as plants in a garden. We are born with good traits and evil ones, and for these inborn traits we are neither to be praised nor blamed. We are no more responsible for them than for the color of our hair or eyes. They come to us by no will of our own, just as an inheritance of property may come to us by legal right. Our responsibility lies in the use that we make of our inheritance, in the culture that we give to our traits. Every one of these traits is as full of thought-germs as a plant is of leaf-germs, and the culture they receive decides whether they are to remain latent, or be developed into leaf, flower, fruit, or branch.

In our judgments of others we are apt to think too little of the power of circumstance in the formation of character; but in our judgments of ourselves we are almost sure to err on the opposite side. We can see quite plainly how our neighbor falls, but we cannot measure the influence that nature, education, or circumstance has had to strengthen his evil propensities, or to weaken his power of self-control. With ourselves it is just the reverse. If we do wrong, we know how hard it would have been to resist temptation ; and we fly at once to circumstance, inborn propensity, education, — anything that we can call to our aid, — as a scape-goat, to carry the responsibility for our sins away from us. Then we do not know how many times our neighbor may have resisted temptation where he has once fallen ; but for ourselves we are ready to say, only this once have I sinned, as though previous resistance to temptation made present failure a venial thing.

The garden, though corresponding truly with the mind of man, is, like all other things and creatures that surround us in this world, separated distinctly from man by being a fixed image, having no voluntary principle by which it is able to make itself better or worse. The plant is incapable of love or hate, and so cannot desire goodness nor shun evil. The animal can only love its own propensities, and hate all that is other than itself, and is as powerless to change its own nature as to alter the color of its skin.

All living things else love and seek only that which feeds their own natural propensities. Man alone can distinguish between good and evil, aside from his own propensities. He alone can see

good and evil apart from himself; and, coming as
it were out from himself, can look at his own
characteristics as if he were another person, and
perceive what in himself is evil and should be sup-
pressed, and what is good and should be encouraged.

The natural traits of every human mind make
up its identity, and we can neither destroy an
original one nor create a new one. All that lies
in our power is to suppress the evil and to encour-
age the good.

We sometimes see a little child who is surrounded by good influences at home seem pure as
an angel, and we perhaps suppose that he has no
evil propensities. The same child goes to school,
and soon seems like another creature,—wild, selfish, and obstinate. Some will say he has been
taught all this by evil companions; but the truth
is, that they have only brought out the latent
qualities of the child's mind. One may as well
guess at what lies in the bottom of an unfathomed
pool, as to suppose one knows the heart of a child
that has lived only in a refined and virtuous seclu-
sion.

So it is with all of us, so long as we live. We
may fancy ourselves pious and kind, if we live

very much by ourselves; but if we go out into the world we are surprised to find how worldly and selfish we are; how irritable, and vain, and envious, and ambitious; how we love to criticise others, and how offended we are at being criticised in turn. The monk in his cloistered retirement, the hermit in his solitary cell, may spend a life in rigid and conscientious self-examination, and yet never learn what manner of spirit they are of.

The world, through its temptations, brings out our latent qualities, and shows us what we are. Retirement lulls many of our qualities asleep, and so hides us from ourselves. The world may take such entire possession of us that we do not stop to see what are the qualities it is developing in our being; but he who truly desires to know what lies within his heart, can hear what it tells him even amid all the confusing voices with which the world strives to drown its words.

In training a child, much time and strength are often wasted in the attempt to change his identity. Instead of trying to find out what his traits are, and then cultivating, modifying, or suppressing them, according as they are good or evil, the parent often tries to create traits, and to fashion the child over, after some model in his own mind.

So in training one's self the same mistake is often made. A model is set up in the mind to imitate, instead of search being made within to see what there is there already to be cultivated or rooted out.

This striving to change the mind's identity is as if a gardener should strive to change not the quality of a fruit, but the fruit itself; to make an apple-tree bear peaches, or a blackberry bush bear raspberries. True, grafting and budding accomplish something of this sort, but only between plants of similar characteristics; and the resulting tree or branch is tender and short-lived in comparison with a well-cultivated natural growth.

If our garden is a level surface, it is idle for us to attempt the imitation of the picturesque beauty of a neighbor's, which is gracefully undulating. If our garden is high and dry, we had better not plant water-lilies in it. We can, to be sure, scoop out valleys and heap up hills, and make a tank where the lilies will grow; but the same labor spent in bringing out the natural capacities of the soil would bring about a far more satisfactory result. There is a kind of landscape gardening, and an abundance of plants, adapted to every locality; and the true grace of nature is brought out with a more pleasing effect where her original capacities are consulted than where they are set aside.

So in the human mind; wise education is the drawing out of the good which lies latent, not the putting in of something foreign. Training is the culture and modification of traits inborn, not the striving to introduce new ones.

We may bring the plants of every zone to set out in our garden, but those only of particular latitudes can live and flourish there. We may crowd our memories with the literature of all times and nations, but only that which finds an answering sympathy in our minds will make its home with us. Once or twice in a century a mind exists which seems to possess capacities so various that it is capable of every kind of culture, as a mountain in the torrid zone may furnish climate and soil adapted to the wants of every plant the earth produces. These are, however, so rare, and so surprising when they appear, that they prove themselves exceptions, and therefore are not to be taken as standards or models.

Circumstance is seldom in our power, but the freedom of our will gives us the ability to make a good use even of the worst. Circumstance is our

great educator; the great power that leads out
the faculties of the mind by nurturing its good
and tempting its evil propensities. It does not
develop our characters so much by shaping as by
simply expanding what it finds within us. The
shaping of our faculties is, for the most part,
accomplished by our own choice and will, after circumstance has expanded them. The beneficent nutriment contained in the wheat is fed by the same
juices of the earth that give their virulence to the
night-shade and the ivy. The same social circle
nurtures charity, purity, and piety in one man, and
envy, malignity, and infidelity in another. The
plant is a unit without freedom. Man is a little
world with freedom. He is not, like the ivy, all
poison, or, like the wheat, all goodness. He is a
garden, stocked with many plants, good and evil,
and he can choose between them, which to cultivate and which to weed out, unless the evil
preponderates so as to make him morally an idiot,
in which case his responsibility ceases.

We cannot too early in life come to a fixed conviction that circumstance is just such an educator
as we choose to make of it. If we are indolent
and careless, it will rule us with the rod of a des-
pot, and bow us down to the very dust of the

earth, till we crawl there the slaves of its power.
If we are earnest of purpose, thoughtful to scan,
and industrious to use the opportunities it offers
us, we may walk erect in the full stature of the
children of the heavenly kingdom, upon the way
that leads to eternal life.

We are often surprised at the effect change of
circumstance produces upon our neighbors, bringing out traits we had not before discovered, or
stimulating traits we had before thought unimportant, till they overshadow the whole character.
Sometimes our friends disturb us by sinking below
the estimate we had formed of them; and sometimes they delight us by rising above what we had
anticipated of them, under the pressure of adversity or the stimulus of prosperity. Looking into
our own hearts we find similar causes of surprise,
both joyful and sorrowful; for probably no person
was ever placed in new circumstances without
finding himself thereby affected in some way that
he would never have anticipated. Yet we are all
prone to think we know how we should feel if
placed where others stand, and are ready to exclaim: "If I were rich as this man, how much
more generous I would be, and how much less
ostentatious;" or, "If I were celebrated as that

man, how much more magnanimous I would be towards my rivals, and how much more kind to aspirants who sought my aid." Imperfectly as we may use our own limited possessions, we can with the utmost ease decide how wisely we should act if more largely endowed, or how much better use we could make of a talent very much smaller than that with which we have been intrusted. We can measure the true relations of anybody's position easier than our own. Self-love perpetually finds some peculiarity in our own standpoint that prevents us from applying the same rules to ourselves that we use for others. Temptation is very easy to resist while we only imagine what its power may be; and the practice of every virtue almost a matter of course as its beauty is revealed before the mind's eye. Yet which of us has a mental garden wherein an unexpected stirring of the soil does not bring the seeds of evil plants near enough the surface to cause them to germinate, and soon to come to a mischievous growth, unless we are ever on the alert to tear them up so soon as they appear. Nothing but the most prayerful watchfulness can save us from falling, if not just as our neighbors do, in ways just as evil. Every soil has scattered through it the seeds of the most divers

plants, and so fast as they are brought near the
surface by culture or accident, they are ever ready
to spring into life.   Just so in our mental gardens,
we can never know what germs of good or evil
lie hid beneath the surface, till the varied discipline of life develops them.

During the ages that have rolled by since the
creation of the earth, the soil has been gradually
accumulating, and burying within itself every
variety of vegetable seed.   Wherever the under
soil is brought to the surface by agriculture it is
soon sprouting with vegetation.   Even the soil
that is thrown out from the depths of mines and
of Artesian wells is often found to be full of these
germs of vegetable life.   In like manner the human mind is compacted from the minds of all its
ancestors.   We inherit the traits of hundreds of
generations ; and not only during this life, but
during the life of eternity, these traits will be
brought to light, unfolding successively as circumstances favor their development.

In unmingled prosperity the mind may lie like
a natural meadow, where rich turf is overshadowed
by stately trees, and nothing unseemly interrupts
the Arcadian picture.   The Divine Providence,
through the discipline of toil, and the common

vicissitudes to which life is subject, breaks up this natural turf as with a ploughshare, and goodly seed is planted; but there springs up with it the seed hidden underneath the turf, and as much care and toil is required to destroy the weeds as to cultivate the useful plants.

Sometimes events come to us like earthquakes, rending the soil, subverting its whole form, and bringing to the light of day things so deeply hidden, that their existence had never before been suspected. Latent wealth of capacity may appear like masses of virgin gold, or less noble metal that with greater effort may be wrought, like iron, to the most useful purposes. And, on the contrary, such a convulsion may cover the before fair face of nature with barren sand.

It is for us to bear in mind that it is in our own power to lay up treasures of truth and wisdom that will be ready to do us good service when the earthquakes come. The mind that has only poverty within its depths is such by its own indolence and indifference. There is abundant treasure offered us by the Heavenly Father, if we will but gather it in. No mind, however finely endowed, has wealth sufficient unto itself; and must sooner or later become bankrupt, if it strive to live upon its own riches, without drawing new supplies from the infinite treasury. The Divine Goodness and Truth are ever coming down to us through the Scriptures, through the workings of Providence in nature and in history, and through the personal experience of every individual mind. Blessed are the eyes that see and the ears that hear. We must look and listen if we would receive of the Divine beneficence; for full to overflowing as it is, our perceptions may be so obscured as to be inaccessible to its influx. As the ivy sucks poison from every variety of soil, so the perverted mind finds food to nourish and inflame its evil passions in every fountain of truth that the Heavenly Father causes to flow for our benefit. That which is a limpid well-spring of sweet and refreshing water to him who seeks heavenly support, is insipidity or bitterness to him who seeks only the excitement that comes from selfish indulgence or worldly applause. The Heavenly Physician stands ever ready to heal us of the infirmities that incapacitate us for the enjoyment of spiritual life; but whatever we receive from Him must be in accordance with our faith in

His power and our love for His person. Those who approach Him only as a good master, and relying in the riches of their own good works, will be disappointed in His replies now as when He was on earth; but those who worship Him as their Lord and God, now as then, will find their infirmities healed and their sins forgiven.

The test of this healing and this forgiveness must be found in the lives we lead, and in the relations we hold to those who are round about us. All that we receive with the heartfelt acknowledgment that it is a heavenly gift, we shall be willing to share with others. The more clearly we perceive that the Lord is our Father, the more ready we shall be to acknowledge the common brotherhood of humanity, and so to give with the same freedom that we receive. Then we shall comprehend how small a part of the virtue of charity lies in almsgiving; and though we may be as poor in worldly wealth as the disciples, we shall, like them, hear the command addressed to us, "Freely ye have received; freely give." We shall learn that we may compel a goodly harvest out of whatever soil may have been intrusted to our cultivation; and we shall be convinced that if the gardens of our own hearts are warmed with Heavenly Love, and watered with Heavenly Truth, they will tolerate within their bounds only such products as spring from, and at the same time nourish, love to God and to the neighbor.